ANCESTORS AND EXPECTATIONS

TALES FROM THE FAE COURT - BOOK TWO

HELLUCY HOWE

STARDUST EMPIRE PUBLISHING

IN THE BEGINNING...

This novella originally appeared in the anthology *A Perfectly Paranormal Halloween*, released in October, 2021.

This amazing anthology is well worth a read - apart from Ancestors and Expectations, there are three other amazing stories to gorge on!

Check it out here:
https://books2read.com/u/3n29xK

To Family, Friends, Fellow Authors and Folks who love Fairy tales.

Thank you.

CHAPTER ONE

DEMAKSIM

A massive elderoak dominated the clearing, its characteristically drooping branches reaching for the sky, the thick, age-whorled bark a rough brown cloak. The sign – Elderoak Tavern – hung from one branch, squawking in every wind gust. Straightening his leather jacket, DeMaksim thrust the door open and strode inside. Conversation ceased. The curious stares of patrons elicited a crawl of goosebumps as he threaded his way to the bar encircling the tree's heartwood. Rolling his shoulders, he wished he could scrub his spine against bark to ease both the goosebumps and his aching wing muscles.

"Whaddya drinking?" A grey leathery-skinned monolith with a rock-solid build and a voice which rumbled like a grating slide of scree, shuffled from the shadows of the trunk's core.

DeMaksim cleared his throat. "Flamuisge, neat."

The flicker of the Rock-troll's beetling brows dislodged a sliver of crumbling shale to the counter top. "Hope yer gut's strong."

DeMaksim chuckled. "What food's on offer?"

One square thumb elevated. "Squirrel stew." A finger joined the thumb. "Two hunks of toasted rye-bread with berries." The second

finger. "Vegies with green dip." A third finger. "Powdered lime-
stone on gemstone chunks." Fourth finger. "Dwarf bread."

"Hmm." DeMaksim rubbed his chin. "The stew, thanks."

"Five coppers the lot."

Reaching into his waist pouch, DeMaksim eased the metal
chips free, pushing them across the polished surface. He was
impressed how quickly the troll's blunt, stony digits nimbly
palmed the coins.

Stubby granite teeth glistening, the craggy behemoth filled a
beaker from a keg, then plunked it in front of DeMaksim. "Grab a
pew."

Holding his mug, DeMaksim crossed to an empty window
booth; his moulded leather trousers slid easily along the wooden
pew. Studying the panes of glass beside him, he decided the name
'window' was a misnomer – years of dripping sap covered any
possible glass. Fortunately, the gloom was lightened by glow-bug
wall sconces.

"May I sit with you, Sir Fae? I dislike drinking alone." A woman
approached his table, her red-lipped smile afire with invitation.
Coppery hair rustled as she swept it artfully behind her.

"Not buying." Set on his mission, DeMaksim was in no mood
for pick-ups.

"I already have a drink." Her wide-lipped smile failed to reach
her eyes as she produced a flask from her shoulder-bag and sat.
"Are you from around here?"

"Thereabouts."

"Got any kinfolk?" She fingered the design etched on her flask.

"Why?" Her questions, especially to a Seelie this deep into
Unseelie territory, raised hackles.

A hiss of laughter. "Just small talk."

The troll appeared, placing a wooden trencher in front of
DeMaksim and a second, larger beaker of liquid. "Water's free."

"Thanks." The delicious aroma of the stew was its own adver-
tisement. Fisting the spoon, DeMaksim dug in. Despite his hunger,
he remained uncomfortably aware of the fidgeting woman across

the table; of her intent gaze, the fingering of her flask, the rearrangement of the burgundy flower nestled in her hair, the trailing of her fingers down her neck, across her throat and down her right breast.

DeMaksim chewed, swallowed. "Not interested."

She frowned. "I'm trying to get to know you."

"I don't want you getting to know me." He spooned up more of the delicious stew.

Pouting, she tapped a finger on the wooden surface. "Just trying to be friendly."

He grimaced. "Take a hint lady – leave."

"Thraxarkzal!" Two dwarves lurched against the table; one with fists in his opponent's beard, jerking the long fibres. DeMaksim flinched as Mr Trapped Beard bit his antagonist's nose and yanked an ear.

"Bezeknazonite!"

"Durkitz!"

Rock-like grey arms yanked hoods tight around dwarfish throats as the Rock-troll bartender – ignoring choked cries – dragged the pair of brawlers to the door and ejected them.

DeMaksim spooned the last few bites of stew, chomping hard on something tough. Rewarded when it popped, he swallowed, grabbing a chunk of bread to drag through the gravy.

A sly smile widened the face opposite. "Good stew?" Lamplight glinted off small, curved fangs. "I thought Fae were herbivores?"

"Look for prey elsewhere."

Her purr was throaty. "I like you."

He tensed. "Go away." Something unpleasant roiled in his stomach; it heaved. Bile threatened. Recalling the tough thing that'd squelched in his mouth, DeMaksim's gaze narrowed on the smiling, over-friendly female fiddling with her hair blossom … again. His lips tightened. "You seeded me."

Hasty fingers dragged red tendrils from her flower – the further her hand stretched, the longer the strands became. Grinning, she cast the threads.

Snarling viciously, he flexed his dagger from its forearm sheath, slicing through the airborne strings. Shrieking pieces plummeted to the table, the strands writhing, blackened where he'd cut them.

"No!" Delicate, curving fangs morphed into vicious, hooked needles.

"Nageen!" DeMaksim vomited, continuing until a coiled pile of snake fell to the table-top. It raised a scaly, hissing head, but DeMaksim called forth a sheeting whoosh of flame, searing the rejected invader and the extra red tendril chunks he'd slashed. Those would've sealed a lesser Fae's fate.

Hissing like steam from a covered billy-tin, the Nageen's eyes slitted, barbed fangs protruding from her suddenly reptilian mouth. Her forked tongue flickered. "But you're just a Fae! Fire isn't possible!"

"Damnation take you!" Slamming fists on the table, DeMaksim spurt-flamed the seeding pod disguised under burgundy hair blossoms. It shrivelled to a blackened wisp.

Screaming, the Nageen abandoned all pretence. It transformed into a large, thick serpent and slithered hastily for the door. The doorbell clanged repeatedly, forced to open and shut for each coil of the reptilian body as she fought to escape. The repetitious sound echoed through the suddenly empty tavern.

DeMaksim retched again.

The Rock-troll appeared, carrying a wooden bucket and a fresh beaker of water which he shoved at DeMaksim. "Good job, Dracon." Using a cleaning cloth he swiped the table several times, rinsing and wringing the cloth between wipes. "She won't be back."

"You could've warned me." Scowling, DeMaksim dragged the back of his hand over his mouth.

The Rock-troll shrugged. "Mate, get real. Ye're in the Dark Reaches. Wasn't sure what she was until she started her play, anyway." His chuckle grated like stones. "Yer handled the rest right fine."

DeMaksim peered around. "Where'd everyone go?"

4

"Out the back door as soon as yer started flaming." The bartender considered him. "She's right, ye look Fae."

"I *am* Fae." DeMaksim snatched the water beaker, gargled and spat the befouled liquid onto the buckled curl of his plate, all the while holding the Rock-troll's wary gaze.

The bartender raised his hands, the cloth dripping down his upraised arm. "I offer no harm, I'm ..."

"A united Queens' man. Their symbol's etched into your arm."

"Damn." The Rock-troll dropped his arms. "Shouldn't have rolled my sleeves up. Yer got a problem with it?"

"Blue blazing hells, no." DeMaksim's smile was wry. "I'm one too." He flipped the collar of his sleeveless jerkin aside, revealing the united Queen's symbol tattooed under his right collarbone.

"Okay then." The bartender nodded.

DeMaksim held his gaze. "Not that it matters, but I *am* Fae; with a few inherited extras."

"Ah, draconic bloodlines." The Rock-troll nodded sagely. "Hard to dilute traces of ordinary Dracons, never mind Primordial Elementals. Gotta name?"

"I'm Mak."

"Good to know, Mak, but I meant the Dracon. Do ye know which of them is yer ancestor?" One lichen brow raised waiting for an answer.

DeMaksim scratched his head. "How would I know if it was one of the Primordials?"

"How long ago was it?"

"Three centuries, give or take a few years."

"Oh?" The bartender resumed wiping the table. "And yer can still flame? Impressive." His hand swept away ash and molten shrapnel. "Need more clues. What'd yer say its name was?"

"I didn't."

"Do yer know?"

"If I did, how would *you* know whether it was a Primordial Elemental?"

The Rock-troll laughed, a rocky booming sound. "It's all in the name, Mak Fae-Dracon. Names are power and there weren't many Primordial Elementals. They came into being when the world was born, are made of the same stuff and will probably be here until the world ends. Or maybe they'll survive. If yer got one of those in yer ancestral line, I'm staying on yer good side. Ye get me?"

DeMaksim huffed a laugh. "Yeah."

"Mind if I ask what ye're doing in the Dark Reaches? Many of the wilder Unseelie Fae and malcontents from the Fae Wars skulk out here."

"Any Draconfolk?"

The monolith's brows arched. More shale shards crumbled down his body. "So! Ye're hunting?"

"Just information." DeMaksim shrugged. "I want to know who bequeathed us the draconic traits; some family members claim it a myth."

The Rock-troll's guffaw shook the table. "Yer flaming ability's no myth."

"Exactly." DeMaksim drank some water. "The idea consumes me; my evolving abilities have created a personal imperative. Queens Dianathke and Maerovana granted me rights to search the royal archives. That's where I found clues suggesting the Dark Reaches as a good place to seek answers."

Dropping the cleaning rag into the bucket, the bartender braced fists on hips. "It's also a good place to find trouble, young Fae lordling, serious trouble."

"Fae lordling?" DeMaksim frowned. "That's a huge assumption."

"Nah, yer dropped the royal names like rain on daisies." The Rock-troll rolled his eyes. "Dead giveaway. Ye're a Fae lordling alright. Out here, yer gotta watch yerself. Letting on yer know either queen can get yer killed."

"Look around you." Lifting the water beaker, DeMaksim saluted the bartender. "I reckon I'm looking after myself right fine, Sir Troll who knows the Queens right well."

The Rock-troll's laughter rattled the sapped-in windows.

CHAPTER TWO

CHERITH

*S*parkling in the afternoon sunlight, the series of interconnected lagoons in a bend of the Mirkdowd River rippled where the willow branches ran twiggy fingers through the tranquil pools.

"You're not wearing weed, Cherith!" Her aunt glowered as she appeared in front of Cherith, her tangled Undine locks, festooned with algae and duckweed, had her niece shuddering.

Cherith Beriaden glided deeper into the largest of the Mirkdowd Pools. "Weed's slimy, messy and makes my hair hard to keep clean. It's not happening, Aunt Brooke."

"Gah!" Brooke pointed to a second Undine just entering the lagoon. "Cascade, you're weedless too!" She snarled, fangs agleam. "You should wear sedge or watercress, not water hyacinth."

"Hi Aunt Brooke." Cascade grinned. "Flowers are so much prettier since Cherry's been working her green powers on them." A third Undine trailed her, webbed fingers swishing through the water in idle circles.

Brooke glared. "Delta, make your daughters toe the line!"

Delta yawned. "Hi sister. Ranting again? We all know there's no line to toe, so back off."

Brooke smacked the water. "We're Undines! We lure travellers to their doom. I lay the disrespect of Undine ways at your door, Delta! You should've drowned the Eldwytch instead of true-mating him and bearing children. Triplets and one male! Whoever heard of Undines producing male offspring? Be glad the Eldwytch claimed the boy. I would've—"

Shooting through the water, Delta erupted in a geyser, digging claws into Brooke's throat. "The boy, Beckett, is my son and Istondir my mate! Do *not* threaten them, Brooke! My choices are none of your business. You don't run this Undine Swirl; we answer to the River King and last time I checked, you lacked the equipment!"

Trickles of pearlescent fluid oozed around Delta's claw-tips, trailing down Brooke's neck and shoulders. Eyes bulging, Brooke raised her hands, the low slanting sunrays glinting off the water droplets dripping down her arms. "Truce sister." Her voice whispered around the chokehold. Hissing, Delta shoved her away, turning to her daughters.

"Cherith, how are you?" Her loving gaze caressed like finest silk. "What have you been doing today?"

Hugging her mother and sister, Cherith grinned. "I've been cultivating the burgundy night-glowing water roses so they'll bloom early."

Delta's eyes swept over her. "I gather the roses aren't out?"

Cherith shrugged. "They're close. I'll go back that way in a day or two."

"Ooh, the water roses." Cascade clasped her hands. "You've such a green thumb, Cherry. May I go too?"

"Of course." Cherith smiled, fingered a strand of duckweed. "I've been working with plants in several backwater lagoons; we can check them all. But first, do you know why we've been called here?"

Brooke waded nearer. "I cry peace sister-kin." Her weed-draped scowl swept them. "I mightn't be the River King but he sent a message – the reason for this meeting. His emissary advises of a Fae-male searching the River Rubiconia on our side, plus all the tributary creeks, streams, lagoons and water glades that combine the Wetland Demesne under the River King's governance."

"That'll take him a lifetime." Delta finger-combed her hair. "Searching for what?"

"The Nixie didn't say."

Cascade tickled the throat of a tiny ruby-spotted frog on a nearby lily pad. "Why'd King Eskavon send us a message? Is there some sort of danger?"

"From a Fae-male? Doubtful. He's in the Dark Reaches, sometimes walking, sometimes flying; we've been tasked with observing him." Brooke's grimace revealed jagged fangs. "It'd be far easier to feed on his magical essence then drown him, but no – we're only to watch and report his actions." She spat. "We're to take turns, a different one of us each day."

Delta rolled her eyes. "Why'd you agree to this, Brooke?" She palm-smacked the water. "Istondir and I planned a few days in the Eldwytch Demesne – we've no time for such nonsense."

Snarling, Brooke flung some weed at the cluster of lily-pads. "If you think I want to spend precious time spying, Delta, your brains are made of fish scales!"

Ribbit, ribbit!

Rescuing the frog from the sudden curtain of weed, Cascade stroked its head, before easing it into the water to swim away. "Maman, you go home; Cherry and I will stay and cover your turn." She looked at her aunt. "Where is the Fae-male?"

"The Nixie shadowed him to that Rock-troll's tavern in the hollow elderoak. He sent a watcher to search for Undines." Brooke grimaced. "He found me."

Cherith sighed. "Damn." She wasn't the least bit interested in spying on some random Fae-male who had little brain – and no sense if he was sneaking around the Dark Reaches – but she'd do what she had to. "Cassie's right, Maman. You go back to Papan and get ready for the trip."

Delta shook her head. "I can't leave you girls to do my share of the work."

"You can." Cascade hugged her. "We're not babies."

Cherith curved arms around her mother and sister. "We're happy to do an extra half shift each, Maman. You go on."

"Alright. We can leave tomorrow." Delta cast sly eyes at her sister. "There'll be no weeds in my luggage."

Brooke glared. "The water weeds disguise us to our prey!"

Delta laughed. "We're Undines with the power to make ourselves blend into the water, Brooke. Weeds are unnecessary. You've never bothered with them before, why now?"

"They add to our mystique!"

"Mystique?" Delta's brows arched. "Are you crazed? Or trying to dazzle a male?"

"Don't be ridiculous." Brooke's lips tightened, but she looked away.

"Aha!" Delta pointed. "That's it! But who would be impressed by weed, I wonder?"

"Just leave it!"

Delta clapped her hands. "I know!"

Brooke swept a wave of water at her sister. "Shut up! Just shut up."

Dodging, Delta grabbed a floating trail of weed and advanced on Brooke. "The Belkaban Bridge Water-troll!" Delta hooted. "That's who. C'mere sis, let me pretty you up with more of this watercress ..."

Brooke back-finned to stay out of reach, but Delta thrust out, her leg-fins flashing through the water as she gave chase.

"I think Aunt Brooke's in heat." Cascade giggled.

Cherith grinned. "Maybe." She cupped a handful of river water, watching as it overflowed around her finger webbing. "Let me know how this ends. I'll go see if this interloper is as stupid as his actions indicate."

Cascade waved. "Okay, I'll see you at shift change tomorrow morning."

~

Moonbeams lit a path across the tree sheltered lagoon where Cherith had made her nest for the night. As comfortable as she could be in a niche at the base of a sweeping water willow, she idled in the water, keeping watch on the Elderoak Inn. The rasp of crickets sounded on the evening air.

Cora-wit, cora-wit, churrr, churrr. The call of a nightjunket carried across the clear flowing stream. A second nightjunket joined in. Calmed by the familiar sounds, Cherith recalled the words of the Nixie whose shift she'd relieved.

The mark's not nocturnal; likely he'll be staying at the inn overnight. There was a dust-up earlier. Roaring and fiery light. All sorts of creatures fled like they'd a ghoul on their tails, including a Nageen in her natural form. Aquinal the Nixie had laughed. *Kind of weird watching her trying to writhe and roil out through the door which kept swinging shut on her.* Aquinal was certain the Seelie Fae-male was still within. *Everyone I spoke to said he hadn't left and I haven't seen him come out.*

Best to make sure. Hoisting herself from the water, Cherith padded alongside one of the well-trodden paths between river-bank and tavern. Slipping from one tree bole to the next, she avoided crackly forest undergrowth, while maintaining a clear view of the elderoak's massive girth. From on high, its glorious canopy swept down in a giant's leafy skirt, while between the leaves, fiery light twinkled through the multitude of windows set into the outer trunk. The welcoming glow gleamed through the gaps around the aged bark of the double doored entry, calling the weary traveller to come inside, rest their aching feet and share a beverage by the warmth of the cheery hearth fire. Cherith wished she could push through those inviting doors in response to the silent invitation, but, ignoring it, she slipped around to the servant's entrance, glancing in every window as she drifted past. To her disgust, ages of dripping sap had glommed-up the windows so all she could see was the warm, but frustrating, internal glow.

Easing down the rear steps into the cellar at the base of one of the gnarled roots, Cherith wondered why she'd heard nothing and seen no-one. Was the place deserted? Aquinal hadn't reported the Rock-troll fleeing, so surely the inn's burly bartender-manager was still here. She crept between two rows of shelves in a room illuminated by glow-bug wall sconces. Shadows reared up over the walls, menacing monoliths of doom. *Quiet, quiet, quiet.* Climbing the two steps to the main level, Cherith's bare feet whispered along the hall until the elderoak's internal trunk – the heartwood – loomed over her. At that central column, she'd a choice of left to the main bar, or right to the stairs winding up to the next level of rooms. The bar door was ajar, the sound of voices drifting from within.

Edging nearer, Cherith was rewarded by the side view of a large Rock-troll. He sat in a pew, feet on a stool as he conversed with someone. Her gaze shifted to a straight-nosed Fae-male with piercing midnight eyes and pointed ears revealed by swept back, shoulder length hair. *Dark hair, nice.* Cherith's anxiety faded. Her target was here and didn't look to be leaving any time soon. She watched for a few minutes, her curiosity roused by the reports, interest piqued by her brief glimpse of the attractive male. What was he searching for? Or who?

Shaking her head, Cherith eventually fell back from her vantage point, retraced her steps, and exited the inn. Once outside, she returned to the stream and her nest between the willow roots where she settled in for the night, her thoughts full of a dusky-haired male with penetrating eyes.

CHAPTER THREE

DEMAKSIM

Chewing on teeth-cleansing mint leaves extracted from his travel pouch, DeMaksim walked the well-beaten track to the nearby stream. He refilled his flask with pristine water from the Mirkdowd. Granite, the Rock-troll, had assured him it was: "clean and then some, because it was birthed in the Mountains of Frashdew and that river's where all my water comes from. Ye've already drunk it." Did his survival thus denote a quality product? DeMaksim chuckled, darkly amused.

Morning light bathed the river bank. He relaxed, basking in the sunrays shining through the undergrowth and beneath the forest eaves, highlighting the leaf-strewn path. It was beautiful, quiet. No bird calls, just the breeze sighing through the trees. Too quiet? DeMaksim frowned. Was he the cause of the lack of animal and bird noise? Wary, he checked under the low hanging branches of the large water willow next to the stream, but saw nothing alarming. Ducking beneath the low, sheltering canopy, he used its skirts to scan outside the tree's leafy domain.

His foray into Unseelie territory might be sanctioned by the Queens, but this wasn't a tame land and possessing a royal pass was of little use if he was foolish enough to get himself killed.

Some of the local denizens would probably kill him *because* he had a royal pass. His search had brought him to the little-known Dark Reaches; the Unseelie gravitating to its depths were often lawless, had something to hide or nowhere else to go. Some were whole clans, like the murdering Redcaps – others were relics and rebels left from the Fae Wars of 50 years ago, in which his father Yanvian, Duke Papillion, had fought. He'd warned DeMaksim: *there are some very bitter and nasty Unseelie with long memories. You can't relax for an instant unless certain of the safety of your environment.* But, DeMaksim's quarry might also be in the Dark Reaches if court archives and Old Venny's translation were accurate.

Stray leaves dropped. Brushing them away, DeMaksim was about to look up when something fluttered in his peripheral vision. Turning towards the movement, he spied a low hanging withy moving like someone had flicked past. Easing forward, he heard a splash as he rounded the bole of the tree – something had been here if he read the flurry of disturbed leaves correctly. At the stream's edge, DeMaksim peered at the water's reflective surface. *X-ray vision would be helpful. Is that a flash? A fish, maybe.* Dropping to his knees, he leaned over the stream, frowning. *Nothing. Did I imagine it?* Further out a waterlily trembled, the pad dipping. He spied a frog and smiled, before refocusing on the wavelets beneath. *There!*

A blurry face surged upwards.

DeMaksim reared back, hands shooting out reflexively.

Hands breached the water – webbed with claw-bedecked fingers – followed by the head of a snarling, green haired, aqua-eyed female. She swiped at him. "Stalker!"

"Not!"

She lunged again; he countered, the fingers of one hand clenched with hers as if they'd agreed to a strength challenge, the other gripping her waist. Her other hand dug talons into his shoulder. She fought to drag him into the water as hard as he struggled to spin her from it. As they wrestled, a ridiculous thought crossed DeMaksim's mind – *classic dance position!* Their bodies whirled, dipping in a frantic frenzy of heat, rhythm and fury.

"No!" The scream shrilled from above. "I saw him first!" The water willow shook as something sizeable thumped through the branches. A Nageen blasted into view, landing at the base of the tree in a violent hiss of slithery coils.

"Blue blazes!" DeMaksim's fight with the slippery, clawing Water Nymph left no time for the Nageen. His startled pause gave advantage to his watery assailant but she also hesitated. *Can I reason with her?"*

"Shtop!" He gasped into the adorable, bat-wing shaped ear. Lisping around his own distended fangs, he inadvertently nicked her lobe, instinctively licking the tiny wound. "I don't wish you any hurt, but the Nageen ..."

The snake woman lunged, knocking them backwards. Her menacing, flared head reared over them, eyes a hellish scarlet. Holding tight to his partner, DeMaksim danced avoidance, while the Nageen whipped cord after cord from a new hair blossom, flinging them in a continuing barrage of scoring red thread.

His water beauty screamed as one slashed her in passing.

That's not happening again! DeMaksim spun, still gripping, and being gripped by, the Water Nymph. Losing balance, they fell, clasped hands swinging high to swipe at a descending red string. Thin scarlet lashed around their close-set arms at wrist height, glowing with feral brilliance as two ends snapped together. Pain sizzled, brief but razor sharp. But they were rolling, the red dazzle fading as the enclosed strands vanished beneath the skin of both he and his river lady. *Shite! Bugger! Demonhells! What's that going to do to us?* DeMaksim's thoughts fizzled as their revolving momentum dropped them into the stream. A colossal geyser of weed and water erupted as they sank in a weird ballet of thrashing, pointed limbs and arched spines.

Wild with panic, DeMaksim surged to his feet, gasped deeply and spat a roaring sheet of red-gold flame at the Nageen, then a second spout of fire and a third. She dodged it.

Unable to ignore the dragging summons of their new wrist-link, his water maiden surfaced beside him, snatched both hands to her chest and splashed some water towards the snake woman. DeMaksim's hand jerked in and out, alongside hers. His mouth fell open as the small amount of liquid the water maiden had pushed, became a mini-tsunami streaking towards the Nageen. *Nifty magic. Is that normal mermaid power?* He spat another fire-blast, only to have it overtaken by the mer-woman's next sheet of water. A powerful ignition occurred, a whoosh of red sparks and green water droplets.

Expecting the liquid to cancel his flame, DeMaksim gaped as the flames strengthened, shimmering from red to icy pale aqua. The watery aqua completely swallowed his burning red flare before continuing to race towards the Nageen with the momentum of a toppling forest monarch.

"He's mine!" The Nageen waved her arms, hissing and shrieking. Her coils undulated, scales glistening oily-olive in the bright sunlight. "I won't let you steal him, you soul sucking Undine!"

"I'm my own!" His voice emerged an indignant gurgle, just as their combined flaming wave crashed down upon the Nageen, engulfing her in a deluge of sizzling, arctic foam. The Nageen's screams were ear-piercing, but she finally subsided, collapsing in crumpled spirals on the river bank.

His jaw sagged. "What the ever-loving shite?"

A violent push came from his right. "Get away from me!"

DeMaksim staggered. "Take it easy!"

The water maiden pulled her left arm in, dragging DeMaksim's right arm along. "Let go!" Their combined hands reached her well-endowed chest.

His gaze dropped and he licked his lips. *What a time to admire a fabulous set of boobs!*

Those aqua-coloured eyes widened. "Don't you try to grope me, you land locked scum!" She batted at his hand. He obligingly yanked it away – her hand followed his. "We're still …"

He flattened his hand against his collar bone – which brought hers along for the ride. Her finger, two, touched the skin of his upper chest beneath his torn linen shirt. *That's nice – better than nice, actually.* DeMaksim forced a frown. "Now you're touching me, river-maid."

She jerked their hands away.

He pulled them back.

Lips pressed into thin lines, she heaved to one side.

Mouth quirking, he tugged the opposite way.

She paused, brows knit in the cutest scowl, delightful chest heaving under some sort of fine brown cloth. "How and why did this happen?" Pretty bat-ears twitched amidst long green locks. "I won't stay like this!"

DeMaksim attempted to ignore the delicious breasts outlined by the drape of her snug, wet gown. *Is it made of some type of weed? Or fabric constructed to look like weed?*

Fingers clicked under his nose. "My face is up here, Fae-male."

Cheeks burning, he met her eyes and recalled the Nageen's red strings of entrapment, one of which had curled around both of their wrists. "I think I know what she did to us."

"She? It is you to whom I'm connected, Fae-male." The Water Nymph – or whatever she was – fronted him, green hair curling as it dried in the breeze, ears tautly upright, voice low. "Release me, now."

"Please, wait." DeMaksim held up his free hand, palm out.

"Grrr!" Mouth stretching to reveal fangs, she darted her head forward, those needles piercing the palm of his hand. She retreated, blood on her smirking lips.

"Ow!" He dragged their linked hands up to his mouth to lick-heal her bite mark. *What's that sizzle?* "Listen, I want to be free too, but the Nageen—"

"Oh, fish dung! She threw those bloody mating strings of hers." Bat-wing ears flickered as she twisted to stare at the river bank. Following her lead, DeMaksim also faced the fallen lump of snake woman. The river girl cupped her free hand around her mouth. "Hey, you! Snake bitch in heat! Free me and you can take him!"

"Thanks for nothing!" DeMaksim growled. "I don't want her, nor am I on the market, or free to a good home. I told her last night when she attacked."

The stream maiden hissed at him. "Not content with spying? Leading women on, too?"

"What?" DeMaksim recoiled. "The hell I'm spying – or hunting females! I'm researching family history."

"Whatever!" She tugged her arm; his moved too. "Come on, if we want freedom, we'll have to get closer to the damned Nageen – and she'd better cooperate."

"Or else?" Despite himself, DeMaksim grinned.

"Else she'll regret it. I have powerful kin." Using both hands, the water maiden hoisted herself up the bank, jerking DeMaksim off balance. They toppled back into the water.

Struggling to stand, DeMaksim felt small, strong arms around his midriff helping him up. *This little dynamo doesn't need kin helping her.* He spat a mouthful of water.

"Sorry, Fae-male. I forgot our link."

He wiped clinging weed from his cheek. "We have to work together, Water-Nymph."

"I'm an Undine, not a Water-Nymph."

"Fine. My apologies Lady Undine." DeMaksim shook water from his hair. "Let's try again. It'll be like a three-legged race, but with arms."

"Three-legged race?" Her lips twisted. "A strange concept, but I think I understand. Wait, what about your wings?" She frowned. "Forget I said that – if you flew, so would I and that's a hard no."

He grimaced. "Doesn't matter. They're soaked through, anyway. Too fragile to lift us."

It still took three more tries before DeMaksim dragged both of them from the water, the Undine sprawled across his back and neck in an ungainly fashion, the arm linked to his stretched to her limit. He lay flat on his stomach; her weight disappearing as she slid off to lie beside him on the bed of old willow leaves under the ancient tree.

Recovering his breath, DeMaksim curled his legs beneath him and twisted to sit, then assisted his Undine. Carefully helping each other, they managed to stand, then approached the Nageen. She lay in an icy, slimy blue-green circle, mouth agape, eyes staring.

The Undine hesitated. "Did we knock her out?"

A sense of foreboding invaded DeMaksim. He prodded her with the toe of his soggy boot – there was no give.

He swallowed, voice emerging a papery whisper. "She's solid!"

"Solid?" The Undine blinked. "How can that be? She doesn't look well, but—"

"Because she's dead." His eyes met the Undine's wide aqua orbs.

"What?"

"We killed her."

CHAPTER FOUR

CHERITH

Staring in horror at the lifeless serpentine body, Cherith shuddered. "How could we have killed her?"

Her hawk featured Fae-male companion studied the body. "Some sort of wave swamped her, something I've never seen before." He swallowed. "I spat flame, but she's not burned; that leaves your water ..."

"Don't gaslight me! She's a solid block of ice, not water! Smoking ice!"

"You can't do ice?"

"No!"

He pursed his lips. "And ice is usually cold, but she isn't."

Bending, Cherith peered at the ground. "Nor is the sun melting her."

"So she's hot but frozen." Green eyes with violet striations met hers. "That's a contradiction, even though I saw your water and my flame merge."

"And?" She studied him. *Vazel eyes! Violet and green is rare and gorgeous. And his hair! The darkness of black lagoon water highlighted by kingfisher blue and wild violets ...* The distant slamming of a door jerked her from foolish thoughts. The Rock-troll was shuffling towards them.

"Lady Undine?" Her towering, lick-able, Fae-male companion frowned. "Surely you noticed our separate powers linking?"

Cherith swallowed. *Oops! Caught mooning.* She jerked the strand of hair wound around her finger. *Ouch! Never mind wanting to drape your-self over him like the water weed Aunt Brooke always harps about. What'd he say?* She searched her memory. *Something about our powers clinking ... No! Linking, that was it, linking.* "Our powers combined. Right! Yes, they did. How? We're strangers – you spat fire and I splashed water."

"That ..." He frowned, delicious vazel eyes pinning her. "Something wrong Lady Undine? Are you wounded? In pain?"

"A few bruises, why?"

"Your expression – such a pain-filled grimace. I thought ..."

"Oh!" *Massive fail in my interested expression, I'll have to practice in a clear pool of still-water.* She stretched her lips into a smile. "No, no, I'm fine."

"Hm." His gaze flashed over her.

Is that a lick of flame in his eyes?

"I'll have to take your word for it." He cleared his throat. "Well, anyway." His focus returned to the dead Nageen. "Your water should've doused my fire."

No, must have been annoyance. I doubt a Lepidopter-fae-male – high-born with that plummy speech – would find a halfling river Undine attractive. But look at those biteable muscles ...

"Are ye both lack-witted?" Granite the Rock-troll stomped through seasons of leaf litter, a sack in one mammoth grey paw. "It's because she bound ye together!" Approaching the body, he sidestepped to see the face. A quick touch to the inert Nageen had him jerking back, shaking his fingers violently, then sticking them into his mouth for a few seconds. Eyes round and wide, he blew on the digits, flexing them. "Well, I'll be! Nasty way to go, but she made her play and lost." From under beetling brows, his stare pinned the Fae-male. "The Undine's power iced yer fire, Mak, or

…" he paused, bowing to Cherith, "… from yer angle, fired yer ice, river maid. Whichever way it happened, the pair of ye look to have turned that Nageen into a block of hot, dry ice."

The Fae-male scratched his head. "But, how does that make sense, scientifically speaking?

"How the scheelite would I know?" Granite glared. "I'm not skilled in sciences, Mak. Are you?"

"Nothing relevant."

"Never mind that!" Cherith hissed. "She bound us with her mating strings. Shouldn't they have disintegrated upon her death?"

Granite's lips twisted. "Yes, but she usually binds a male to her; instead, she bound her male of choice to another female." He plucked at a trail of lichen hanging from his ear. "It's outside my understanding." He frowned from Cherith to Mak.

Mak barked a laugh. "So, none of us has a clue what in demon-hells actually happened? The Undine and I should've negated one another! I'm fire, she's water …"

"And I'm rock!" Granite hooted. "Was the Nageen paper or scissors?"

Mak threw his hands high, perforce dragging Cherith's left one with it. "Frigging demon-hells, Granite! This isn't a game!"

"No, it isn't! And you're going round in circles." Cherith jerked her arm down and flicked all her fingers, spraying the stupid-arse males with water. "The Nageen's dead! Her damned entrapment strings should've disintegrated with her. Now we'll have to break the threads ourselves. Pull your arm back in opposition to mine Fae-male!"

He did, but the invisible cords stayed firm, allowing no leeway. "It's not working."

She bared fangs. "How very observant!" *River Goddess! We've pulled and twisted and wrenched and wrestled – do NOT think about the wrestling with his hot body, Cherith!*

With his left hand, Mak reached to his hip, producing a dagger. "This will work."

"Be careful!" Cherith screeched. "You can't see—"

"Now who's being obvious?" He glared. "Of course I can't see, but I've other senses. I can *feel* what I'm doing." Easing the blade between their snug wrists until he met resistance, he sawed back and forth.

"Is yer dagger blunt then, Mak?" Granite's brows drew together. "Nought looks to be happening."

Mak grunted. "It's bouncing off." He pressed harder, but only succeeded in forcing their united wrists downward. Frowning, he sheathed his blade and checked the strings. "Blue blazes, they're not even damaged."

Cherith ground her teeth. "So you and I are stuck together, Sir Fancy Pants Fae?" *What in the black lagoons is going on?* She rounded on the Rock-troll. "Granite, any thoughts, or answers, would be acceptable, about now!"

"I'm not a freaking Oracle, river maid." Arms akimbo, the Rock-troll glared; shale chips trickling down his face. "Why don't ye find one and ask them? Better yet, ask yer King!"

She glared back. "How would King Eskavon know?"

"Well, he's older than you, for a start. Older than me. And, he's *yer* King, not mine."

"Quit arguing!" Mak considered the Rock-troll, cocked his head. "Granite? Those little bits of rock that keep falling off? In the interests of science, do Rock-trolls ever flake away to nothing?"

"Holy River Goddess!" Cherith flicked more water at the dolt. "You're both idiots! Rock for brains and a pretty spy who should still be wearing a swaddling cloth!"

"I'm not a blasted spy! I—"

"You've been seen poking around stream banks and traipsing through backwaters." Cherith glowered. "You're looking for something, or someone, and my king knows about you."

"Wow! I've been observed and reported to your king?" He snorted. "Tell me who's spying now?"

"Don't try your pathetic reverse psychology on me!" She bared her fangs. "I'm not the invader."

"Nor am I." He opened his mouth, closed it and scrubbed his

scalp. "I'm simply a traveller touring the complete Fae demesnes and I enjoy exploring waterways."

"Scheelite." Granite turned away, shoulders shaking.

A hoot of laughter burst from Cherith. "That's frog shite! Nobody comes to the Dark Reaches on a scummy holiday." She shook her head. "That's a one-way ticket to hell. Try again pretty fae."

"Why?" He thrust his face towards hers. "It's my business, back off."

"Linked remember? Now it's my business too." Cherith snapped her teeth at his hawkish looming nose.

"Don't you dare!" Mak reared back.

Lurching forward, Cherith fell against him. "I'm over this!"

"On that we agree." His other arm wrapped loosely about her, firming around her waist, his balance steadying, holding them upright.

She held his frustrated gaze. "Let's both stop waving our arms, call truce and work together to break the Nageen's magic."

His fingers gripped her hip, flexed. "A truce is an excellent idea. So is breaking her magic – I agree."

She nodded. "On that note, I'm Cherith – you're Mak?"

He smiled. "Yes …"

An explosive snort burst from Granite. "By the Rock of Ages, ye're a hard-headed pair. About time ye realised ye'll work better as a team."

Mak's mouth bared, revealing even white teeth, the small fangs of the Fae-kind indenting his lips. "You're so helpful, Granite. We wouldn't have coped without you."

Cherith laughed.

"I might be a Rock-troll, but sarcasm ain't lost on me, Mak." Granite hefted the sack he'd brought. "Ye left yer pack behind and I lugged it out, but I can throw it in the river."

"Okay, sorry." Mak's scent was redolent of pine mixed with the delicious tang of bark leather; Cherith couldn't grasp why she wanted to bathe in it. "We need to find someone who understands what's happened."

"Another Nageen would know." Granite shuffled closer.

"We'd have to reveal we killed this one." Cherith shuddered. "I doubt they'd be happy, so – no, not happening."

The Rock-troll shrugged. "Just listing options." He tapped Mak's shoulder, raising the pack by its strap. "Stop cuddling and lift your arm, Mak."

River Goddess! We are *cuddling!* Cherith took a hasty step away.

Mak grimaced, but extended his arm, allowed Granite to position the strap over his head and across his body. His gaze rose to meet hers. "I meant neither harm nor insult."

Cherith rolled her bottom lip between her teeth. "Okay." She smiled weakly. "Supporting each other is a good idea, and not just physically. We need to be fully cooperative to sort this out."

"Agreed." Mak's brows tightened. "So, let's compare suggestions on what to do next."

"Or where to go from here." The rumble of Granite's voice was lost in a loud splash. Water cascaded over all three of them.

"Unhand my sister, Seelie monster! We've been warned about your kind!"

Oh fish crap! Cassie's here for her observation shift.

CHAPTER FIVE

DEMAKSIM

*D*eMaksim stiffened as a second surge of liquid hit, cold after the sun's warmth. The water became steaming foam as it crashed over the solid statue of the dry-iced Nageen and sizzled on its return path to the stream.

"Cascade Lystreniel Beriaden! Stop that at once." Cherith glared over DeMaksim's shoulder. The rain of water ceased.

"My full name?" Cascade whistled. "You must be okay. Why are you and the spy hugging, Cherry? What's with the dead Nageen? Aquinal said nothing about a body."

"Well, the body's a bit recent-ish." Cherith grimaced. "And we're not hugging. The Nageen tied us together. We were discussing our next course of action when you arrived."

Eyes like saucers, Cascade straightened. "Hopping toad's freckles, Cherry! This was supposed to be simple; watch the spy and see where he goes …"

Turning himself and Cherith, DeMaksim bared his fangs. "I'm damned tired of being called a spy! Sounds like you lot are spying on me!" *Shite! My fangs are larger than usual. What's caused that?* He glowered at the females. "You lot need to butt out of my business." *What's that tingling in my fingertips?* Lifting his free hand, he saw a scaly paw with deadly hooked claws at the tips. *Blue blazes, that's new! And pale blue-green scales instead of mid-brown. Am I evolving?*

Cascade slammed hands to her hips. "What in the name of the River Goddess and all her fishy offspring are you?"

Tongue lolling thickly, DeMaksim hissed. "I'm Fae!" Smoke curled from his nostrils.

"And a whole lot more, Sir Fae-not-Fae."

"Cassie, you're not helping." The shake of Cherith's head dragged silky green locks over DeMaksim's scaly skin. The strands snagged before sliding away.

Arousal twined through him.

"I'm trying to protect you, Cherry!"

"Well back off. I'm a perfectly capable adult."

"I'm older than you—"

"By two minutes! You're being ridiculous."

"Give it a rest!" Granite held both huge hands up. "We just finished arguing and now ye've started again. Nought will get done at this rate."

Cascade folded her arms. "I'm simply trying to understand the situation."

"Well, the Nageen bound these two together with her mating threads. The strands should've disintegrated upon her death, but—"

"You're mated to this creature, Cherry?" Cassie's mouth rounded to an 'o' of horror as she stared at DeMaksim's pale turquoise scales and claws. "Why, he looks draconic, not Fae! I thought Dracons were extinct?"

Cherith glared. "He's not a creature; his name is Mak and we appear to be linked. We're trying to work out how to break the binding."

Granite guffawed. "Ye can't believe everything ye hear, Undine."

Cascade's mouth thinned. "I think I can help." She waded to the bank. "If you'll allow it?"

Cherith relaxed. "Of course, Cassie."

"Your help is appreciated." DeMaksim rumbled. He watched Cherith's sister exit the water and approach. Cascade smoothed both hands down her hips; one vanished within the folds of her skirt and reappeared clutching a strange looking, conical blade. He stared in disbelief as her fist reared. Cherith screamed as the point descended towards his chest. Then his wits returned and he dodged, roaring as anger swamped him. A ball of flame rose in his gullet.

"No!" Cherith surged forward, swinging between her sister and himself.

Cascade shrieked as Cherith plunged into the path of the swiftly falling blade, trying to pull back.

Fire bubbled in the back of DeMaksim's throat … *Too close! I cannot hurt Cherith.* Head aimed high, he belched his gout of flame skyward, tilting off balance as Cherith's momentum tugged him inexorably in her wake. They crashed into the retreating Cascade, tumbling into the river in a thrashing, contorting, intertwined threesome. Light faded as water closed over his head and he sank. A foot to the kidneys, hair in his eyes, fingers jabbing the back of his knee, the sharp sensation forcing him into a spasmodic lunge upward. Sunlight leered tauntingly through filters of liquid, gyrating bodies and waving weed.

Surfacing, DeMaksim gulped breath, then was rolled under the water again. His Undine-tethered wrist wrenched him deeper; he came face to bulging eyes with a balloon-fish. The creature shot away between some reeds as he flailed, wallowed, was jerked over and around, saw the flash of a finned leg and tried to hold his breath. His mind kicked into gear. With his free hand he felt along the arm connected to his until he rubbed against a female form. *Cherith!* Firming his grip, he kicked hard to bring both their faces into the air. A dripping Cascade bobbed up nearby, spluttering and wailing. He glared, but she was no longer intent on him.

"My Narwhal blade! I've dropped it." She dove under the water.

Karack, karack, karack. The grinding clatter of rasping rock assaulted DeMaksim's ears, a continuous stone-on-stone grating.

Is that an earthquake? The ground's not shaking. Seeking the source of the rasping discord, he swept water from his eyes and identified Granite howling with laughter on the riverbank.

The Rock-troll pointed. "That was the best thing I've seen in a shale's age! Yer faces! The lot of ye writhing like a slither of eels!" Another burst of crushed pebble-mirth erupted from his craggy mouth. "Life was boring before ye came to the Dark Reaches, Mak. How long can ye stay?"

"Shut it, Granite." DeMaksim massaged his forehead. Ignoring another burst of ear jarring rumbles, he focused on the weight sagging against him. Cherith's eyes were wet with tears, her chest heaving. He forced himself to avert his gaze from temptation. "Cherith? You alright?" Her scent was unfamiliar to him, but delicious all the same.

"S-she m-meant to k-kill you! I'm so-sorry. I-I didn't know."

He rocked her. "It's fine. Her blade missed me when you—" He tensed. "Cherry? Did the knife connect? Are you hurt?"

"A scratch." She wrinkled her nose. "Nothing to worry about."

But he did. Turning her, he searched until he located the scratch beneath her unfettered forearm. Swallowing, he stared at the wound she'd taken protecting him; a cut leaking pearlescent fluid in a filmy trail along her delicate flesh. Hand shaking, he raised her arm gently to his mouth and licked the wound clean, tasting her skin, her blood, the essence of her being. The sweetness of tending to her felt satisfying. *Because of the Nageen binding?*

"Stop!" Cherith's mouth trembled. Her entire body shook as she pulled her arm away from him. "I'm alright. Y-you shouldn't do that, but thank you."

Blinking dazedly, DeMaksim cleared his throat. "Right." His gaze returned to the river. "What the blue-blazes ails your sister? She crazy?"

"I don't think she properly understood." Cherith tongued her bottom lip, staring at the violent eddying where Cascade searched for her precious blade. "She's not usually violent, but she likely thought she was rescuing me from an untenable situation."

"Not violent?" His laugh held no mirth. "She's wielding a dagger."

"I know, but ..."

Cascade's upper body appeared; she was brandishing her blade. "I found it!" She arrowed closer, stopping when DeMaksim flung up his left hand.

"No nearer. This isn't my day to die and you've already slashed your sister."

"Oh no, Cherry, I cut you?" Cassie's ears drooped. "I'm so sorry."

"What in blazes were you thinking, Cassie?" Cherith's voice shook.

"To free you from the Nageen's binding!"

"By killing Mak?"

"Well," Cascade reasoned. "He *is* holding you prisoner."

"He's not, we're trapped together!"

"Oh!" Cascade bobbed her head. "My apologies, Mak."

Growling, Cherith pointed. "And just where did you get a Narwhal tusk blade? Why in surging whirlpools do you need it?"

"I got it from Old Venny, the tinker trader, last time he came through." Cascade shrugged. "It called to me, I couldn't stop stroking it and I couldn't leave it there. So I traded for it."

"Traded what, exactly?"

"It must have been something good. Old Venny drives a hard bargain." De Maksim remembered past bargains.

Cassie's head dropped. "The hairpiece of grime-roses you made me."

"What? Cassie how could you? Do you know how much time it took me to cultivate those grime-roses, harvest them at the perfect moment and make that hairpiece?"

Cassie pouted. "I'm sorry. I really am, but I had to have this tusk."

"Fine." Cherith sighed. "May I see it, rather than feel it's edge?"

"As long as you keep your hands away." Cascade gripped the conical blade and clutched it to her bosom. DeMaksim couldn't help where his thoughts went. *Pretty, but from what I've seen so far, Cherith has nicer handfuls.*

Cherith frowned. "You know the Narwhal must be dead for you to have that tusk, don't you?"

Cuddling the knife like a lover, Cascade rolled her lower lip between her teeth. "I don't sense violent death on this blade – nor any death actually."

"That can't be right." Cherith peered at the gleaming spiral shape. "What Narwhal would give away its horn voluntarily?"

"I know it sounds crazy, but there's no death link. There's emotion of course; the love for family, the sensations of everyday life, the bravery of defending oneself. But the strongest is a deep sense of longing. For what, I can't sense, but," Cascade shook her head, "feelings of dying are just not here."

"A puzzle for another time." DeMaksim massaged his temple. "You mentioned Old Venny, the tinker trader – he gets around further than I knew."

"Yeah." Granite smiled, revealing nubby grey teeth shaped like square blocks. "He carries an amazing variety of goods. Always has the right thing, sometimes it's something ye never knew ye needed until he shows ye."

"Goods and information." *Lucky for me he was visiting Queen Dianathke's castle and was able to help me decipher the archaic Eldwytch writing in that old scroll which contained accounts of Dracons.* DeMaksim pursed his lips. "When did you see him, Cascade?"

"A few days ago."

"Hmm." *After he left the castle then. I spent ages searching for the easiest way to get through the tightly tangled scrub bordering the Dark Reaches and he probably knew a way – should've asked him when I had the chance.* DeMaksim rubbed his chin. "Which way did he go? He mightn't be too far away; his advice might help us get free."

"Oh, yeah." Cascade gestured in a southerly direction. "He went upstream. Oh wait! Cherry, that flower which counteracts Nageen venom, maybe it'll work on those entrapment cords?"

Cherith's brow cleared. "That's a great idea."

31

DeMaksim focused on her. "Where do we find this flower?"

Cherith sighed. "We'd need an Eldwytch mage, like my Papan, to create a potion from them, but it grows a fair way upstream."

"You mentioned King Eskavon might be able to assist – where's he live?"

"Upstream." Cherith and Cascade spoke simultaneously.

"And the deeps of the Dark Reaches?"

"Give ye one guess." Granite winked.

DeMaksim winced. "Right." Dragging his free hand through his hair, he tilted his head towards Cherith. "I've a suggestion then – what say we head upstream?"

"That's brilliant Mak!" The grate of Granite's laughter assaulted their ears. "I knew as soon as I saw ye, last night, that yer pretty head housed useful grey matter."

DeMaksim flipped him off.

CHAPTER SIX

CHERITH

"You'll need help collecting the anti-venom flowers." Cassie's fingers flexed on the hilt of the Narwhal blade, her expression hopeful. "I'm free to join you."

Cherith shook her head. "No you're not. You need to tell Aquinal to cancel the watch rotation and bring Papan up to date so he'll be ready to prepare the potion we need when we return with the blossoms."

"Oh, yes! I can do that." Cassie grinned. "I'll go right now." She waved and dived into the river, surfacing a fair way out to wave again before she swam away.

"Thank you." Mak stared after Cassie until she was out of sight. "That saves me from having to watch my back."

Cherith huffed out a breath, not certain whether she was more annoyed with Cassie or with Mak. "I did it for me, not for you. Cassie has a way of finding trouble and we've got enough already. Shall we get going?"

"Absolutely." Mak turned to Granite. "Thanks for your help. I'll not forget."

The Rock-troll nodded. "Happy to be able to assist. Drop in any time ye're back this way." He turned towards the inn, stumping briskly, and was soon out of view.

"This way." Refusing to look at Mak, Cherith tugged on their link, her brows drawn down. *He'd better not be difficult.* Without a word, he fell into step beside her and they set off upstream.

～

Flanked by the old-world guardian forest, the river rippled and basked in the afternoon sunlight. Cherith was not in a mood to appreciate the lovely vista. She usually swam her way along the river, but being tied to Mak forced her to walk. *Damn land-dwellers!* A couple of hours of blasted foot slogging and her feet were paying the price. She sighed, bending to massage her right foot and flip away a pointy pebble. "I'm not used to all this land walking. The ground's so hard."

"Should have considered your bare feet sooner." Mak frowned. "We'll get into the water."

"That'll be harder for you."

"I can wade, or swim, as needs be."

"Swimming will wet your wings again." Cherith rolled her top lip. *His wings are so beautiful; the lilac, blue and green splotches glow against their sooty backdrop and are petal soft under my fingertips.*

"Wet wings aren't painful – your feet are." His gaze warmed. "I could fly us both?"

"Oh, no, no, no. You'd be carrying me." Her ears wiggled as she looked up at the sky, eyes huge. "That'd strain your arms or your wings."

"Strain me?" Eyebrows skyrocketing, he stared. His lips formed an 'o'. "You've never flown! Of course – you're nervous?"

She swallowed. "Sorry."

"It's okay." A calm smile. "What if we walk on the softer ground at water's edge?"

Hunched shoulders relaxing, her head tilted. "For me to be on the water side of our pairing, we'd have to cross to the other bank."

"Yep. We'll get wet again no matter what." He shrugged. "I'm guessing you need water to survive?"

"Yes, but not as much as true Undines – my father is Eldwytch. An Eldwytch green mage to be precise."

"Ah." Mak nodded. "Must be where your growing thumb comes from." He indicated a water willow stretching long branches low over the river. "We could sit on that branch, have a snack, and bathe our feet before we cross."

"Thanks."

His look turned serious. "Before we let this flying idea go, Cherith, I'm advising you I'll take us both to the air if I deem it necessary."

"It will be unnecessary." *The Mirkdowd river territory is home – what could possibly make it dangerous enough for flight? He needs to see the niche I've carved for myself – despite my differences, I fit in.* "I'm going to share something." Leading him to the willow's trunk, Cherith laid palms on the ancient bark. "Copy me." He frowned but capitulated, twisting his linked hand. "Now close your eyes and focus on the tree. See inside to the heart where time and sap flow slowly." Verbalizing for Mak's sake, she eased her essence along the tree's veins, gradually forming a connection with the water-willow. "Oh mighty willow, greenly growing, your branches, leaves and roots sweeping the water, the ground, the sky, I offer you a heart check in return for permission, for my companion and I, to sit on one of your branches and rest weary feet." The tree responded with a golden surge of warmth. Broadening the channel, Cherith drew on her green power, encouraging the flow through the tree, from trunk to root, then branch, node, leaf and bud. Near the base were signs of a grub infestation, which Cherith scorched with an intense burst of vibrant emerald; her power had never come so easy or been as clear. The willow shivered, then bathed them in golden radiance. "You're most welcome, lovely willow." She patted the bark affectionately and eased free.

"I felt that!" Mak was wide-eyed. "All of it!"

"I wasn't sure whether you would, but the Nageen's link seems to have opened a few doors between us." Cherith smiled. "It's such a beautiful feeling helping plants be healthy."

"You're more Eldwytch than Undine?"

"By nature." Her smile was rueful. "In looks I'm Undine, in skills I lean to Eldwytch green magery like Papan. It's Beckett who looks truly Eldwytch – whereas, Cassie and I don't. We lack Undine natures though. Our parents say looks mean nothing, but most people judge by appearance, expecting us to behave true to our appearance."

"Looks like one, must be one." He rubbed his jaw. "Do Undines really drain souls?"

"They can. Some of the nastiest do." Cherith wrinkled her nose. "I literally can't – I physically lack something, for which I'm grateful. The idea of draining souls sickens me." She shuddered. "My power promotes growth, life and strength." She shook her head. "The opposite to what Undines do."

"What you showed me with the willow indicates a healer. Is it just plants, or can you heal people?"

Her brows shot high. "I've never thought along those lines, I only work with flora. What if I can help people?"

"You were the green flow?"

"Yes! And the willow gave back golden warmth – did you feel it?"

"I did." Smoothing a lock of hair back, his gaze was thoughtful. "You could try healing your injured arm. It's not bleeding, but there's still a wound."

"My arm!" Excitedly, Cherith sourced her power, the swirling green pool of magic she'd always shared with plants, maximizing their health and growing abilities, then thought about her arm healing. Her fingertips did their familiar tingle, but the cut remained a cut. "Oh! It didn't work." She looked at Mak, disappointment choking her.

"Hmm." Mak frowned. "How do you normally make it happen?"

"I usually draw it up in ribbons until my heart is full, then aim my hands at the plant – it flows down my arms and out through my fingertips."

He cocked his head. "Wouldn't you need to send it around your body instead?"

Cherith curled fingers into her palms. "Of course! I don't want it exiting; something needs to push or pump it through me … Wait, my heart!" Excitement rising, Cherith visualised her power as a green ribbon linking with her blood, flowing out from her heart, circulating through arteries to her extremities and returning through her veins. The sensation was a warm spreading glow. When it reached the area of her slashed arm, the warmth intensified to nearly a burn, fizzed for a few seconds, then faded and continued on.

"It worked!" Mak held her arm, lifted to expose the slash site. Barely a line remained where the wound had been, fading even as they watched.

"River Goddess." Cherith shook her head, eyes riveted to the now unblemished skin. "This is amazing. I've always been a plant nurturer. As a toddler, I'd stroke them and talk to them – afterwards the plants would be better, stronger, grow larger than usual, provide more beautiful blossoms. Everyone said I was a natural with plants, a glorified gardener I suppose. There was never any idea my magic could work on people too."

"Restricted by expectation." Mak's mouth twisted. "I know what that's like."

"You do?"

"Part of the reason I'm here. I've lived my life dancing to the expectations of others; I decided to find out whether that shape really embodies me or whether I've blighted myself by trying to be what everybody wanted." He glanced around. "Come on, let's settle onto the willow branch and talk about it over food and foot soaking."

"That sounds great. Who's going onto the branch first?"

"Well, we're traveling upstream." Mak gestured. "With my right wrist bound to your left, I have to lead with my left side and we must be on the far bank for you to be in water."

"True." Cherith nodded. "You'd better lead."

"Okay." Climbing to the low hanging branch of the willow, left arm spread for balance, Mak stepped carefully onto the branch road. His linked hand stretched back, fingers clasping Cherith's, as she eased along behind him. Jacket riding higher with his outstretched arms, he kept his Lepidopter-fae wings tightly furled. Underneath, the terrain changed from grass to sandy bank, reeds, then the clear swirling water of the river, deepening as they progressed.

Keeping her eyes on Mak's moving form, Cherith stepped instinctively, her feet feeling the branch. *Looky, looky at that nice tight butt in those cuddly leather pants, Cherry. Uh-mmm.*

Mak's voice reached her. "There's a nice shaped part of the branch ahead, that'll make a good seat."

There sure is.

He looked back, smiling encouragement as he continued stepping. Suddenly, the smile vanished, his eyes went impossibly wide, his mouth opened. "Aargh!" He toppled backwards, one arm windmilling, the other attempting to, except she was attached to it.

"Mak!" Jerked from her feet, Cherith fell to the branch, encircling it with her free arm, grasping as tightly as possible. Mak disappeared into the river beneath her. Their arm-link dragged, her hand tickling the water's surface, but she dropped no further. *Thank the River Goddess! We're holding. He'll be able to use me as an anchor to climb out. I hope he's okay – the Mirkdowd is so muddy on the bottom here.* The water roiled. What was going on? *Maybe I'd better go in and ...*

The agitated water parted. Glistening in the sunlight, a huge winged creature erupted skywards, bellowing as it soared. The roar blasted through the atmosphere, deafening Cherith. Quivering, she closed her eyes and tightened her grip, but it wasn't enough. She was wrenched screaming from the branch and dragged into the sky. Wind whistled around her lower limbs as she hung limply, secured only by the tenuous threads binding her wrist to that of ... Mak?

CHAPTER SEVEN

DEMAKSIM

*D*eMaksim choked on a mouthful of water and weeds for the third time that day and was completely unprepared as deep inside, his alter ego snarled, ripped open a previously unknown internal door and bucked into the driver's seat. *Wh-at's this?* His bewilderment allowed the other him to settle; his body jerked, expanded, changed and arrowed for the surface.

Bursting from the water, DeMaksim shot skywards; an exploding supernova with outspread wings, head and limbs thrust out like the arms of a five-pointed star. His bowed back forced his chest forward, his face aimed high and jaws agape for the release of an outraged roar. A gout of icy-green flame sheeted to the heavens; huge curls of fire accompanied a second roar. The world went silent, the forest hushed … until far away, from the depths of the Dark Reaches, a fainter ululating bellow was heard.

An echo? No, a challenger! Hovering above the water, DeMaksim craned his neck, switched his scaly tail, and opened his jaws to answer.

"Mak! Mak is that you? Oh, River Goddess, it must be – the wrist link still holds." The voice distracted him.

I hear a female. His head spun. *I smell a female – my female! Where?*

"Mak!"

A tugging on his right front leg. Before he could look, something shrilled and spat in his face. Jerking back, he fought to focus in close. Clinging to the sparkling curved horn on top of his long snout was a catfish. "Mrrrow!" It shrilled again, head butting his horn – *I have a horn?* A light thwack-thwack-thwack across his snout; the catfish assaulted him with tiny clawed fins. "Mrrrowww!" The catfish glared. DeMaksim glowered back, hissed, tilted his snout and flicked. "Mrrrooowwwwww ..." The catfish sailed off, tumbling towards the river, squalling as it fell. He hissed; why hadn't he eaten it? Maybe he would. There was time—

"Ma-a-k." A soft shaking voice, more tugging, weight on his leg. His gaze ran down the scales of his right foreleg.

"Erp?"

"Mak!" A green haired female clung to him, limbs wrapped around his thick foreleg. Gorgeous aqua eyes huge in her sweet, golden skinned face, she was tied to him with red cord around the lower joint of his foreleg. He stared.

There is a female on my foreleg. Foreleg? Shouldn't that be my wrist? And why do I have a snout, a horn and scales? His huge scaly tail with its fan-shaped end lashed as he tried to get a grip on reality. *Tail! I have a tail? Am I dreaming?* His brain reeled, mind working furiously. Facts, he needed them.

"Mak?"

Yes! Mak. No, not Mak, DeMaksim. That was it – he was Heir-Lord DeMaksim Yanvian Aphiski, a Fae-male, eldest child of the Duke and Duchesse of Papillion. His soot-black wings and hair, splashed with lilac, soft blue and grass green, identified him as being of the Swallowtail line of the Lepidopter-fae. His life, his circumstances, rushed back to him, a tornado of thoughts and images swamping his mind.

"Dracon – Mak, please focus."

Blinking, he recognised the little aqua-eyed, golden skinned darling with pert lips and ears mimicking the shape of bat wings as Cherith Beriaden, his—

"Mate?" The word lisped from a mouth that felt strange. He worked his jaw, tried again. "We're mates?"

She grimaced. "Yes, well, the Nageen force-mated us. Remember?" She shook their combined wrists. "It's false, even if all the mate stuff is happening to us, any changes will disappear when her cord does, right? We can't see it now, but it's—"

"Red." Drawing his Cherith decorated foreleg close to his chest, he cupped the claws of his other foreleg around her.

Her brilliant smile returned. "You remember! Thank the River Goddess, I thought you lost to the Dracon body-snatcher."

"Remember? No, I see the string." Wrinkling his snout, he struggled to form words through elongated jaws. "And there's no Dracon body-snatcher, just me. I'm DeMaksim, as I've always been. Though never quite like this." His tongue poked out, testing fangs, sweeping across lips that were not familiar. "What in blue blazes is going on?"

Cherith tilted her head. "Are you alright?"

He shook himself. Water droplets flew. "I think so; maybe." He eyed the sky in which they hovered. "Let's land and talk." Snapping his wings, he took them higher, twisting and banking without conscious thought, performed a wobbly glide towards the further river bank and back-winged to an awkward landing. *Shite! I flew. Without even thinking about it.* Unused to the centre of gravity in his current body, plus female leg decoration, he stumbled a few steps. *Erk! This body is so ungainly.* Recovering, he glanced around at the sandy river bank; it ended in a low bluff which looked to be a few steps away. But when he moved his new larger body reached it in one stride. Freaked out, he tried not to think about how different he was, tried to ignore the inner voice yelling in alarm … Who was he?

Settling onto his haunches, body upright but leaning against the bluff, he brought his cupped and linked fore-legs, cradling Cherith, to one huge knee so that she faced him. Lowering his head, DeMaksim studied her intently, curled his new, powerful wings with their trailing edges of feathery fronds into a protective curtain and created a private niche. Sun bathed the leathery skin; it glistened in a pearly opalescence of aqua, blue and green.

"Look at you!" With her free hand, Cherith stroked down his gleaming foreleg to a three-digited paw, tested the sharp claws, then found their connecting rope. "Why isn't the Nageen's cord hurting, despite your arm's increased size?"

"I really don't want to look at me, right now. This is crazy." DeMaksim shivered. "As for the cord, it must have stretched?"

"Gah! It doesn't stretch – we tried that." She stared at him.

"Well, it has. Why are you staring like that?"

"You're so beautiful!" Her gaze drifted over him.

"I am?"

She nodded. "Your eyes are still vazel, but the rest of you is aqua and green and blue. Your head is scaled and feathered, you've got twin green, spiral horns between simply gorgeous feather-tufted ears, a curving crystalline horn on top of your snout and look how big your nostrils are!" She twisted, looking further. "Then your jaw arches back to your neck in such an elegant way …" She touched a fingertip to one of two large fangs curving down from his top lip, drew her finger over the lower lip, then stretched up and kissed the side of his snout. Staring at the place she'd smooched, she kissed the same spot again.

"Err." He drew his head back, inexplicable warmth flooding him. "What's that for?"

Cherith giggled. "That catfish was funny – your eyes criss-crossed looking at it."

He huffed. "Fierce little thing; but how did that lead to kisses?"

"It cut your nose." She folded her lips, looking sideways at him. "I made it better. Kissed the boo-boo."

"Boo-boo?" A laugh jerked from him. "Haven't heard that term for years. Brave of you to kiss this fierce hulking creature." His eyes widened. "Blue blazes! I'm a creature! A Dracon! What am I going to do?"

"You're not a creature!" She glared. "You're Mak. And you need to calm down."

"How do you suggest I do that?" Nothing in him felt calm.

"How about we talk this through?"

He shuddered. "Don't know how talking is going to help."

"It's a distraction. Think of it like a story."

"This isn't a faery tale."

"No. But you already know a lot about me, so it's time to reciprocate."

She peered up at him, such expectation on her face he couldn't disappoint her. "I suppose it's worth a try." He let out a gusty sigh, his breath blowing fronds of hair back from her lovely face. "Okay. I'm DeMaksim Aphiski, heir to the Seelie-Fae Duchy of Papillion."

"Ha!" Cherith prodded his broad scaly chest. "Seelie-Fae; we were right."

He glared. "But not a spy." Flexing a claw, he stared at it wildly, then averted his gaze. "Although I *am* a Queens' agent, I'm also really here on a personal mission. All our lives ..."

"Our?"

"Oh, I'm the eldest of seven. After me come three sisters. Lyssica, Janeska and her twin Tindresse, then my brother Treymeron and my two youngest sisters, Armelle and Zhulija."

"Wow, your parents are prolific."

He snorted, then froze as steam issued from his nostrils. "Shite! I'm, I'm—"

"You're fine, Mak." Cherith's smile was soothing. "We were talking about your parents, yes?"

He nodded. "Oh, that's right. They say we're delightful expressions of their love."

"How sweet."

"Sweet, right – if Maman could just see – no. Better that she can't see me – It'd be better if I couldn't see—"

Cherith grabbed his foreleg. "Stop, Mak, it's okay."

He rolled his eyes, gulped. "Anyway, Maman says we've

draconic blood from her family line and, sometimes, the talents of family members reflect that."

"Tell me more." Cherith tilted her head. "How does it show up?"

DeMaksim swallowed. "Okay. Um, usually, Fae exhibit basic magic abilities until puberty arrives and that's when our main gifts start to develop. There can be physical idiosyncrasies because of mixed bloodlines …"

"What do you mean?"

"Well, I've sensed something extra inside me, because when I became emotional – angry or upset – I showed some scales. That's classed as a mixed bloodline physical idiosyncrasy; a small thing with no real use." DeMaksim frowned. "I've always been able to produce scaled sections of skin at will, emit bursts of flame and my fangs could enlarge. Since meeting and being linked to you this morning, it's more. Suddenly I'm breathing out steam or smoke, or something and my hands turn into clawed paws."

Cherith rested her chin on a fist. "And this afternoon you changed – hmm, let's not go there again." She frowned. "What is this 'basic magic' you spoke of? It's not a term we use."

His eyebrows rose. "Basic magic's part of our genetic make-up; the innate ability to be graceful, to connect to the world of which we are a part, harnessing the natural energy that flows through and around us, to manipulate it in small ways – depending on our personal strength and even our imagination. It stems from our querencia."

Cherith tilted her head. "Querencia?"

"The internal place from which our strength is drawn, where we feel most at home, most our truest self. It manifests differently in everyone – I'm excellent at organising, strategising and some-times being able to subtly influence things. Perfect skills for being the heir to a Duchy with lands and people relying on continued prosperity. I was always expected to be heir, not because I'm the eldest, but because of those qualities." It had always made him wonder if anybody saw the real him.

Cherith pursed her lips. "So, for me, such skills would naturally be water and nature-linked, based on both my Eldwytch and Undine heritage?"

"Without the Undine soul-sucking ability."

She shuddered. "As I said earlier, I'm so glad I wasn't in that queue. It's a curse, not a skill. The very idea revolts me."

He shrugged, immense shoulders rippling, scales flashing sunlight. "We are what we are."

"I guess so." Cherith sighed.

He eyed her morosely. "Until we're something more."

"And a very handsome more, too." She winked. "Now, what's this 'personal mission' you mentioned?"

"Oh, that." He followed her lead. "For All Hallows' Eve, everyone in our family gains a closer connection, to tradition and our forebears, by researching an ancestor. When the All Hallows' Eve ritual takes place, we each tell the family about our choice of ancestor and light a candle for them. The candles burn all night – the time when the veil between worlds is thinner and spirits may visit. The candle is to light their way home."

"What a lovely tradition." Cherith smiled as if entranced. "I'd like to do that if I ever have children."

He smiled. "It's nice. Last year, Zhulija asked Maman questions about the draconic link." Grimacing, DeMaksim tilted his huge head. "Zhu can magically alter temperature and uses heat in her artwork without being heat-affected, making glass and sculpting metal. She asked if Maman knew who the draconic connection was and where they fitted into the family tree."

"Did she?"

"Maman said not, but that seeded in me a want, a need, to know what truth the rumours held and I began investigating."

"A subtle push from your inner self?"

"Maybe." DeMaksim shrugged again. "I started the next day, investigating all our records, before I visited Maman's parents, Grandmaman and Grandpapan Neptulidae, and scoured their library. Clues pointed me to Elrodel, the palace of Queen Dianathke and then to Queen Maerovana's Castle Synternesse.

Both of those castles originally belonged to old King Oberon and I obtained permission to search the archives for draconic references and any information on the Neptulidae line – Maman's family." He tapped a claw on his bottom lip, remembering the rooms and rooms of old books and scrolls in both castles.

"Keep going." Cherith swirled her hand. "What'd you find?"

"Initially, fleeting references to Dracons, similar to things Maman mentioned. Grandmaman spoke of a cousin named Mel, who'd gone to be a royal attendant to one of the older queens, that's how I ended up at the royal residences." He shook his head. "There's so much stuff in those archives; I spent lots of time there. Nothing about anyone named Mel Neptulidae – that dead-ended – but the Mel part could've been a pet name, I suppose. I found a scroll written in old Eldwytch which Old Venny helped me translate."

"Old Venny the tinker trader was there?" Cherith arched her brows. "I wonder how he came to be fluent in old Eldwytch."

DeMaksim chuckled, amazed to discover that her plan had worked – he had calmed and a sense of rightness settled over him. "I asked him that. He said he'd been snowed in, up in the high country one frost season many years ago with an Eldwytch elder who had some old scrolls and he'd little better to do than learn."

"What was in the scroll you found?"

"It listed and described Primordial Elemental Dracons."

"Primordial Elemental Dracons?" Cherith's brows knitted. "What are they?"

"Old Venny called them the Elder Dracons." DeMaksim grinned. "In the wise words of Granite: 'there are a limited number of Primordial Elementals. They came into being when the world was born, are made of the same materials and will probably be here until the world ends. Or maybe they'll survive.' Quote unquote."

"Wow, I wonder how many exist?" Cherith nibbled her bottom lip. "And why that sent you into the Dark Reaches? I don't see the connection."

"The scroll mentioned that Draconfolk had withdrawn from the known world, and had last been heard of migrating into the deeps of the Dark Reaches."

As if on cue, a faraway bellowing rose and fell and rose again, before descending and trailing off in a drawn-out moan. The nearby forest noises hushed.

Cherith's eyes rounded. "What was that?"

CHAPTER EIGHT

CHERITH

"Could've been anything. Maybe even one of those lost Draconfolk." Mak shrugged, the motion causing feathery face-fronds to fluff about. He stared upstream from whence the moaning roar had originated. "Maybe we'll find out; we're going that way."

"It was definitely something and I'm not certain it sounded happy. In a fight? Issuing a challenge?" Cherith shook her head. "Probably better if we can avoid whatever it was. There are lots of very nasty Unseelie-Fae; I'm normally not a target, but you're an interloper in Mirkdowd territory and that changes things. We need to be wary."

Mak continued watching upriver. "No argument from me."

Brushing at the filaments tickling her cheek as his jaw worked in speech, Cherith caught a soft strand around her fingers. Pausing, she studied the pale aqua length in arrested surprise. "I thought these were fine feathers, but now I see they actually resemble a water fern which grows in some of the backwaters. What kind of Dracon are you, Mak? If you don't mind discussing it now?"

His faraway gaze refocused, those gorgeous vazel orbs intent.

"Er, yeah, I'm okay, I think; but how would I know what sort I am?"

"Oh, I thought your scroll might have described some Dracons." Tilting her head, Cherith twisted and stretched to study him. "You said you've manifested scales in the past?"

"Yes." He eyed the paw curled around Cherith, deadly claws pointing. "They were brown."

Her eyebrows rose. "Yet now you're this pearlescent greenish blue colour with gold-edged fronds looking like trailing weed, have rippling ferny fins, a spiny tail and you belch green flame."

His jaw worked. "Last night, defending myself at the inn, it was red flame."

Cherith's right hand fisted. "That means the changes have happened today." She swallowed. "Since the Nageen bonded us."

He huffed, producing steam? Fog? Smoke? "In comparison: you have aqua hair, gold skin with a smattering of freckles, green eyes, fern-like fins on the backs of your forearms and lower legs, webbed ears, fingers and toes."

She felt the blood drain from her face. "So you're developing watery characteristics in my colours because of our forced link?" *This can't be happening – surely we're not mated for real?*

Mak swept a forked tongue over his lower lip. "If that's the case, wouldn't you be taking on some of my features?"

"Oh, good point." Cherith looked down at herself. "Nothing's changed."

"Apart from your wave of water turning into ice."

"It was your draconic heat that turned it into hot-ice."

"Just as your water changed my red flame to green." One claw scratched his head. "How can hot, dry-ice exist? And how can water and flame combine?"

Her hands turned palm upwards. "No idea. Didn't we cover this earlier?"

"Yeah, so if we're going round in circles, it's a good time to move on. Thanks for helping me calm down." Stretching, Mak stood; continuing to cradle her.

Looking down, Cherith gulped. "Um, Mak? I believe it's time to change back to your Fae-male self, especially if I'm to walk in the water."

"Ah, about that." His mouth thinned and he looked to be fighting down panic. "I can't shift."

"What?"

"I've never been full Dracon before today, so I'm not certain how it works." He grimaced. "I've been trying to change back while we talked. It's not working."

She stared. "But you said you bring on scales at will – how do you, ah, get rid of them at those times?"

His lips twisted. "I withdraw my will and they fade."

"Try that then."

"I have." He looked away, embarrassment darkening his aqua cheeks. "Only, this time wasn't my choice to change – I didn't even know I could – I think withdrawing my will is failing because—"

"Oh, you didn't will it in the first place." Cherith grimaced. "Okay, walking won't work if you can't shift. I'm already smaller than your person shape, but even tinier compared to your Dracon."

"Exactly." The stretch of his mouth revealed sharp teeth. "There's no choice, we'll have to fly."

"Fly?" Her voice was a screech of horror. "No!" *Goddess-goddess-goddess!*

"Come on Cherith, it'll be fine." Tilting his head, Mak batted dark lashes over his beautiful eyes. *Not noticing those eyes. How come I never knew how much I love eyes that colour? Didn't see how long his freaking eyelashes are, either. Nope.*

"I flew us to the riverbank safely, didn't I?"

"Because I wasn't expecting it! And flying means we'd be in the sky!"

"Well, yes. We can't fly if we're not in the sky."

"Stop sounding so reasonable!" *There's nothing up there. No support. Not like when I'm surrounded and supported by the river.*

Mak huffed, feathery weed-fronds swirling. "You cannot seriously expect me to shuffle along the riverbank at an excruciatingly weird angle, just so you can wade or swim in the water!"

Cherith glared, then pictured what he'd said and dissolved into giggles. "That'd be so funny!"

"You think?" He glowered. "These wings differ from the swallowtail ones of my Fae-form, but they're still wings and I've been flying all my life."

"But it's air! There's nothing to hold you up!"

"My wings do that. I work them, use the wind and air currents, the same way you do with your arms, legs and fins when you're in water."

Fish poopers. That makes sense. She noticed him grinning. "What?"

"Your ears were wiggling madly, but now they've kind of drooped – you've given in."

"Oh, really?" Cherith reacted instinctively, surging to her feet. She tried clapping palms to hips and glaring, but her bound left wrist twisted against Mak's foreleg, refusing to cooperate. "Dammit!" She bared teeth, attacked where the cord felt firm around their limbs. She couldn't see the string, but it's rubbery texture in her mouth was foul when she fought to grip it in her tiny fangs. *It keeps sliding free. Does the bloody stuff have a mind of its own?*

"By the Queens!" Mak's body shook with laughter. "You know that isn't going to work, Cherith. We couldn't separate the strands earlier no matter how hard we tried and now they're visible, they don't look at all damaged."

She stilled, her mouth releasing their wrists; her eyebrows shot up. "You can see them? It must be because you're in Dracon form."

He nodded. "Yes, as soon as I morphed to Dracon they became visible."

"It doesn't help, though." Cherith dropped her head into her free hand. "What's it going to take?"

"We've got a plan, Cherith. Don't give up." Mak's scaly but soft cheek rubbed comfortingly against hers. "We're going to harvest the antidote flowers and ask your father to brew a potion."

"You're right." She sighed, soaking up the support. *He feels so good.*

"But to do that, we've got to find the plants."

"We're back to flying again."

"Yep."

"But have you flown with a passenger? Me as extra baggage could, um, you know, put you off."

"I just flew with you, so your arguments are pointless." He arched a brow. "You fit cupped in one of my paws or, if you prefer, you could straddle my fore leg – your size isn't a significant factor here."

"I might fall."

"Now you're being ridiculous." Lifting his right front leg had her dangling in the air, before he lowered her back to his propped knee.

Her head sagged. "Damn. I *am* being ridiculous. Sorry."

"Flying will save us lots of time." Mak tipped his head. "Plus, the quicker we harvest the anti-Nageen plant, the sooner we can ask your father to make a potion to break this forced mating, yes?"

"Absolutely. Yes. You're right, of course." Sucking her bottom lip between her teeth, Cherith worried at it. *He wants to be rid of me. I can't blame him. We're not mates – and yet, something about our connection feels right. I want to keep him. Is the Nageen's magic affecting me?* She shuddered in confusion, then shook her head. "Yes, well we're not mates so we deserve to be free of each other."

"Agreed."

"To get on with our lives."

"Yes, so flying?"

Cherith blinked, swallowing hard. "Okay, but hold tight, please."

"Always."

Did that sound like a vow? Filing it away for later consideration, Cherith began wriggling into a position she hoped was safe, wrapping herself around Mak's foreleg, facing forward. "I'm ready."

"Okay." There was a lurch as Mak's heavily muscled back legs bunched and launched them. His wings beat strongly as they ascended. Cherith's stomach was pleased that he didn't go high. Levelling out several feet above the treetops, he followed the line of the Mirkdowd's channel. His voice rumbled, somehow still audible to her despite the wind of their flight. "I thought if I stayed low, you'd find it easier to guide us."

"Good idea." Her breath sawed in her throat, threatening to choke her, but Mak kept his wing-flaps even, their speed moderate as they swept upriver, avoiding the banks and the bluffs, plus any looming trees or growths of reeds and bulrushes. After a while, Cherith relaxed, feeling safe enough to enjoy the experience. When the river angled left and they winged around the bend, her stomach didn't lurch even once. *Yes! I've got this!* In this section, trees crowded closer to the water's edge and Cherith admired how the surface glowed in the late afternoon sunlight.

Mak bent his head towards her. "We need to stop for the night. Know anywhere close suitable for both of us?"

"If you don't mind roughing it."

He snorted. "Done that many a time – as long as it's safe, it'll be fine."

"Just ahead on the right there's a wide lagoon with an island in the middle."

Following Cherith's directions, Mak found the island, located a clearing amidst the tall, dense shrubbery and back-winged to land. Folding his wings he glanced around, noting the stand of trees overhanging one side of the clearing. "Now what?"

"There's a shallow cave with an overhang in amongst those trees. You won't manage the cave, but you'll fit under the overhang."

"Okay." Shambling forward, he made his way between tree trunks and strange shaped boulders until the cave and the over-hang came into view. He settled onto his haunches with his right side next to the cave and lowered his right front leg for Cherith to slide off. The surrounding trees obscured the westering sun; the light was dim. "I did have some food in my backpack, too bad I've lost it somewhere"

"We could fish; the river's on our doorstep. Come on, I'll show you the most likely places. The fish love to hide under snags in deepish pools near the bank."

"In that case …" His hunger persuaded him and by the time they'd finished fishing, it was fully dark. Mak charred the fish with his new green flame, and they ate on the riverbank before returning to their campsite.

"Have you wondered why the Dracons came to the Dark Reaches?" Cherith asked as she finished her fish, settling deeper into his cupped paw.

"Ever since I understood the scroll's information."

"And you're looking for them? What do you hope to find out?"

"The name of my draconic ancestor for one. Maybe the reason why, after all this time, I'm who and what I am. Why did the Draconfolk come into the Dark Reaches and withdraw from the known world? The Fae demesnes are home to many and various creatures and species, so what's the problem with Dracons being in the mix? Were they diseased? Maybe there's no problem and they just prefer to be hermits, but they've left behind offspring who need help and answers. I believe there's a duty of care, but maybe being primordially immortal implies that caring is beyond them. Only, where does that leave me? Should I vanish somewhere too, now that I can become a Dracon? If there was a disease, maybe I have it or can contract it." His pause was filled by the whirr of crickets and the sough of the breeze as it danced among the leaves of the trees outside the overhang. "I'm hoping those answers might help me discover I'm not just the child who is expected to take over the Papillion Duchy after my father and whether I still can."

"You're looking for a sense of self, then." Her breath warmed his skin. "Me, too. I've struggled with looking Undine but having an Eldwytch nature. I've learned to accept who I am – a nurturer of plants, the environment and life in general; none of that is Undine."

"You don't hide yourself; that's what I've got to stop doing."

"Why did you? Isn't your family loving and caring?"

"Yes, they are." He sighed. "As my draconic traits emerged, I worried that I was too different, too volatile to be an acceptable next Duke of Papillion. Seelie Fae society has certain expectations of their nobility, so I hid those differences as best I could and forced myself into an imitation of my wonderfully successful father. Until I felt like an impostor in my own skin, someone I didn't even recognise. That's when I knew I had to do something and the All Hallows' Eve ancestor research gave me the excuse I needed." He wrinkled his nose. "This is really weird – I've told you stuff even my family doesn't know. Was there more to the Nageen's bewitchment than her tying us together and instigating the changes we've both had?"

A look of horror crossed Cherith's face. "By the River Goddess, I never thought of anything like that. What if you're right?"

"Then our problems just got bigger." He sighed. "Also, I promised my family I'd be back to participate in this year's All Hallows' Eve celebrations."

"Oh, but, isn't that in two more days?"

"Yes."

"So what will happen if you fail to keep your promise, Mak?"

He blew out a breath. "They'll assume I didn't show because something's wrong and send out search parties."

CHAPTER NINE

DEMAKSIM

*W*aking to find someone sprawled atop him, DeMaksim blinked into a sleeping face he'd decided was unfairly adorable. Cherith's lips were slightly parted, one cheek squashed the fastenings of his leather jacket into his chest, her other cheek rosy in the dawn's light. Tousled strands of hair feathered around her ear. Her left arm hung to the ground over his right side, dragged by their link, while her right arm stretched down his other side. Elegant fingers grazed the indentation to the left side of his stomach, just above the waistband of his pants. He swallowed, hardening against her hip despite trying to ignore the scorching heat of her fingertips through the linen of his shirt. He cleared his throat, chest vibrating.

Cherith murmured, rubbing her cheek against him, her face scrunched sleepily. Reaching to shake gently, he stilled, staring at familiar sinewy, long-fingers. *Blue blazes! I'm no longer Dracon! How in demon hells? And I still have my clothes – that must be part of the morph-magic, otherwise I don't understand.* His attention was snagged by Cherith yawning, her mouth a shapely curve of enticement. Stiffening everywhere, he forced himself to relax, body part by body part. He was almost done when Cherith wriggled and his relaxation technique failed him … *morning wood, it's just morning wood. Will you get a frickin' grip! OMG! Grip?* He palm-heeled his forehead, thrusting away the image his thoughts had engendered. Huffing, he rubbed his face, fingers digging into the sinuses above his brows and thumb punishing his cheek. Pretty green eyes opened a slit, met his, then widened.

"Mak! Look at you – you're a person again!"

"A-huh, just realised that myself." His voice was a croak.

Cherith reared up onto her knees, sliding between his rapidly spread thighs, to inspect him with smiling delight. "That's great!" She faltered as she noticed the unmistakeable long thick bar near her knees and blushed. "Oh! Um, how did you do it?" Her blush deepened. "Er, change shape I mean." She clapped a hand to her forehead. "River Goddess! From Dracon to Fae-male – how did you do that?"

He grimaced, choking on his amusement. "Er, I slept?"

"Right!" She nodded vigorously, looking anywhere but at his groin. "That makes sense."

His eyebrows arched. "It does?"

"Yes! You became Dracon under emotional stress, but when you slept, you relaxed and – snap! Things happened." Cherith's thumb and mid-finger clicked together.

"Yeah, snap. Makes a crazy kind of sense. So does returning to my Fae-male shape."

Cherith clenched her eyelids shut. "Duckweed! I don't think I'll ever speak again."

He laughed. "Sorry. It's too easy to tease you. I guess feeling normal again has lightened my spirits."

Her eyes opened and she grinned. "That's good, Mak. Really good."

Deliberately, DeMaksim drew his legs in, moving to his haunches; it reduced the distance between them but eased the strain on their linked wrists. He looked away from her happy smile; it still smacked his chest and soaked through his skin. *What is she doing to me? I need to protect her, want to kiss her and have the*

58

strongest urge to keep her. The reason washed over him. "Ah, it must be the Nageen's binding."

"What?" Cherith cocked her head, looking doubtful. "I doubt the binding has anything to do with your overnight return to being a person, but I could be wrong. And you still have your clothes. Shouldn't they have been torn to pieces or something? I know that happens to other were-animals." She frowned. "So many questions. We need to find a Dracon so that you can get the answers."

Taking advantage of her misconception, DeMaksim sighed. "We can't blame her for everything, I suppose. Too bad." He massaged his chin. "Locating a Dracon would be perfect, but our chances are slim."

"Why? They were here once; we just have to find out where they went."

"My grand plan in a nutshell." DeMaksim nodded. "But they disappeared for a reason and mightn't wish to be found. Plus, right now it's more important to sort out the mess the Nageen created. My Dracon hunt will have to wait." His belly rumbled. "Did we eat all the fish last night?"

"Yes."

"Okay then, food on the run. How far are we from the flower field?"

"The antigeens are in a meadow only a few more hours upriver." Cherith scanned the sky beyond the overhang. "We should start; there's cloud building and we have to walk now."

Standing, they selected the path between the trees used the previous night and arrived on the island's narrow beach within a few minutes. DeMaksim checked the remains of the picnic they'd shared, but now, not even the fish heads remained.

"Do I want to know what the local scavengers might be?"

Cherith shrugged. "Probably crabs. C'mon, let's walk to the tip where the lagoon branches away from the main river." Keeping to the firmer sand just above the water's edge, they began walking. DeMaksim's calf-high leather boots scuffed heel and toe marks in the sand, but Cherith's bare feet left barely a mark. DeMaksim wasn't happy leaving a trail, especially with all the unknown dangers being this far into Unseelie territory brought – besides, it went against all his training – but there was little he could do. Dragging a branch through wet sand would be just as obvious.

The beach ended at a stretch of rocks which they picked their way through to reach the point. Although the Mirkdowd was still wide here, DeMaksim's keen eyes noted a narrowing of the riverbed further upstream. The current was gentle, the water diverging around the small island sprawled across the lake's entrance, bifurcating the river. Either side of the island were narrow channels, the river's entrance to the wider, shallow lagoon.

"Do you still want to do the walking-wading thing?" DeMaksim peered at Cherith. "I have wings in my Fae form too." He spread the black appendages with their cream, lavender, blue and green markings.

"Oh, they're so pretty!" A soft breeze stirred her hair as she twisted to see them. "I'd heard most Seelie Fae and some Unseelie have lepidopter wings, but yours are the first I've seen. Swallowtail butterfly?"

"Correct."

Her eyes took on a faraway dreamy look. "Cassie once saw the Unseelie Beast, Lord Dario Eribifax. He swept through here, hard on the heels of a tribe of murderous Redcaps. He has wings of the Dark Crimson Underwing moth in crimson, black, silvery-grey and cream – Cassie said he was absolutely delicious. I was sorry I missed it, despite the threat of those vampiric Redcap parasites." She sighed, returning to the moment, but her pleasure faded as she met his gaze. "What? Something wrong?"

He rolled his eyes. "Dario Eribifax just true-mated and married my youngest sister."

Her eyes widened. "Lord Dario? And um, Zhulija, I think you said?"

"All the way out in the boonies of the Dark Reaches and still touched by family." He shook his head, forcing a chuckle while choking down the useless feeling of wanting to punch out his brother-in-law because Cherith was drooling over him. *I'm pathetic. Even worse, I know my feelings are all a false construct brought about by the frickin' Nageen and yet I still can't help it.*

"Wow!" Cherith's face glowed. "He found his true-mate, that's so romantic."

"Yes, it is." His voice emerged deep and gruff. "They're beautiful together."

Her eyes rounded. "But he's Unseelie and she's Seelie!"

"Yep, but they definitely true-mated and the union was embraced and blessed by both the Fae Queens."

"How wonderful." Cherith's grin lit a fire in the centre of his chest.

"I agree." He rubbed his burning sternum. *Thank the goddess. She's genuinely happy for Zhu and Dario.* Seeing it helped him overcome his unwanted filthy jealousy of the new brother-in-law he truly liked. "Back to where we are, however. Will you fly with me?" *Demonhells, it sounds like I'm asking her on a date.* Heat flashed up his neck and face.

She tapped her lip with one finger. "Just to the other bank? Because, I really need a soak in the water – I'm not usually out of it for as long as I have been."

"Oh, of course!" DeMaksim smacked his forehead. "Do you feel okay? We'll hurry across, then wade and walk as we originally planned, before my draconic change."

"Thanks." Her smile warmed him. "It's really not far to the antigeen flower field. It won't take us long."

"Let's go then." DeMaksim spread his Fae wings, put both arms around Cherith – which hobbled her, but she hugged him around the neck with her free arm – and flew them across the river. Hunger had them stopping to nibble on berries and some kithgreens they found and Cherith managed to catch an inquisitive fish.

DeMaksim considered the medium-sized fish. "I wonder if I can flame-cook it without changing shape?" He laid the fish on a nearby rock. "Previously, my skills weren't that good." Pursing his lips, he blew a stream of fire, pausing at one point to turn the fish over and blow some fire at the raw side. He gestured between Cherith and the cooked fish. "I did it! Dinner is served Milady."

Cherith laughed. "Breakfast, more like, but I'm happy either way." They shared the hot sweet meat as they continued traveling. When the riverbank ascended to a higher bluff, one of them had to give way on their preference. DeMaksim, thoughts of his mother's glaring lecture on manners surfacing, joined Cherith in the water, despite her protestations.

"Your boots!"

"They'll dry. Really, they're fine. They've been dunked in water several times since we met and still function, whereas your feet are bare and there could be rough ground or prickles up there."

Despite his words, DeMaksim was secretly pleased that the water remained shallow enough to only cover the heels and soles of his boots. He was more than happy to keep his leather pants, leather jacket and linen shirt dry also, and crossed his fingers in the hope they would remain that way.

Part way through the afternoon, Cherith indicated a side tributary on their left; a small rill burbling down a narrow rocky staircase in an area of extended high bluffs. "We have to go this way."

"Up the stairs?" DeMaksim eyed the pathway between the broken cliff edges.

"Yes, then backtrack along the water course."

"How in the Queens' name did you find this place?"

Cherith grinned. "Curiosity. The idea of stairs intrigued me enough to investigate. I've been up and down this river, explored all the banks and tributaries, checking out the plants, cultivating them. I know it fairly well."

"That helps."

"For instance, there's an unusual paved area in a hollow up there. It's on the opposite side of the streamlet, across the antigeen meadow. It looks like an entry, or a gateway, with paving between two garden beds leading to some steps."

"Where do the steps go?"

"Nowhere. They culminate in a small grassy plateau which runs into a cliff after a few seconds and that's all."

"Huh." DeMaksim scratched his jaw. "That is weird."

Cherith nodded. "The entire meadow is a bowl, a valley surrounded by cliffs. It's like someone planned to build a home there, but the paving and the steps is as far as they got. You'll see." She turned to lead him up the rocky flight of stairs, their feet shushing through the shallow water to one side, but avoided the splashing of the main water supply.

DeMaksim shook his head. "It would've been easier to fly."

"But not half as much fun." Cherith smiled over her shoulder.

CHAPTER TEN

CHERITH

*M*ak shaded his eyes against the sun lowering in the sky. At the top of the streaming stairs was a narrow canyon between higher cliffs, bisected by the little creek's flow. Although the channel gradually widened, the cliff on their left side curved away from the stream-bed to frame a small bowl-shaped pasture. It continued to circle behind the meadow in a continuous wall and became the backdrop to a large stand of trees. On the right side of the stream, a wall of cliff climbed in a series of ascending ledges.

"A beautiful but out of the way place. We getting out of the water here?"

"We are."

"Great." He took a step towards the open field. Grinning, Cherith pulled on their linked arms.

"Not that way." She pointed up. "We're climbing."

"Isn't the meadow easier?"

"Yes." Cherith turned towards the cliff. "But I've been growing increasingly concerned with your safety. I know I said we'd have nothing to worry about, but I've decided to be extra careful anyway. This valley is very open and I'm not the only Unseelie to know about it. I travel a lot and most places are fine, but there's something about this out of the way mountain meadow that always makes me uneasy. I'm not foolish enough to think everybody is friendly – this way I can check the lay of the land without being seen." A cleft in the rock provided footholds to a narrow ledge which widened as they traversed it, snaking at an angle up the cliff wall to a wider crevice. The larger gap was an entrance into an enclosed rocky channel with stone walls rising up each side, much like that of the stream bed.

"At least it's dry underfoot."

Cherith giggled. "You and your boots."

Mak winked. "I have wings – my boots aren't used to rough treatment."

"What are they made of? Reeds and mud?" A reverberating blurt from behind had Cherith whirling. "Did you just blow rude air at me?"

Mak's eyes were wide and innocent. "Me? Why ever would I do that?"

"Because I called you out on your unnatural fixation with a pair of boots, maybe?"

"Unnatural fixation!" He clapped a hand to his chest as if he'd been stabbed. "Harsh."

Cherith's laugh was cut off by a distant roar. She frowned, looking up towards the rocky peak they aimed for. "Come on."

Mak's voice was a low murmur. "Was that from the meadow?"

"Maybe. I need to see." She jogged, Mak keeping pace. The path turned a corner, opening out to a wide ledge with a clear view of the bowl-shaped valley. "Stay low." Cherith went to her knees, Mak quickly hunkering down beside her. She scanned the meadow, the whole of it a panorama beneath them, some areas more shadowed in the lateness of the day.

Warm deep breath tickled her ear. "I can't see anything – you?"

She shivered. "No." Her gaze swept back and forth. "Those trees are the usual place people go and the only real concealment."

As they watched, a hare shot out of the undergrowth beneath

65

the tree line, darting to open ground; a squash-faced Goblin chased it. Cherith gasped, Mak tensing beside her. The creature's strands of grey hair wisped out from under a red hat, fangs protruded from both upper and lower jaws as it leapt after the hare with a four-footed crabby gait. Eagle-taloned hands ripped and tore at the ground, sending clods of turf up in gouts as it galloped in pursuit. Howling, the goblin dived, digging its claws into the hide of the fleeing animal. Snatching the squealing hare close to its chest, the creature lifted its face to the sky and howled in bestial glee before falling, fangs distended on the hapless hare. The animal's blood-curdling scream was drowned out by harsh laughter as another goblin cleared the trees. Slurping noises followed.

"Redcaps!" Shuddering, Cherith dropped flat to the ground, Mak beside her.

A grating voice drifted to them, adding to the ruckus made by the feeding Redcap. "Hare, Malkurx – want some."

"Hunt own, Grisbore!"

"Why no share?"

"Lazy scuz, Grisbore!" a third voice hissed. "I hunt, you watch for Fae-male and water girl."

"Idiot, Vantark! They no come, Malkurx too noisy." In the fading light, the two goblins faced off as they argued.

They're looking for us? Mind whirling, Cherith nudged Mak, voice a whisper. "Go back the way we came."

"Sun's almost set." Mak breathed in her ear. "I don't fancy a downwards climb without light. Is there anywhere to hide near the paved area you've mentioned?"

"No."

"We're better off staying here, then."

Cherith's hand clasped his in a quick tighten and release. They stayed low, watching the Redcaps.

"Alright Grisbore." Vantark made a slashing motion with his claws. "Snack here, go back down river and search. They near." The goblin snorted. "Seelie Fae stupid not to use wings and she just half-breed Undine – no threat. Easy as Snortgrub's sister. We have soon. Tastier than rabbit. We give to River King, then he let us eat." They both sniggered.

"They're leaving." Cherith crossed her fingers, watched the shadows darkening more every second until the sun disappeared below the horizon and night moved in. The darkness veiled the goblins' antics, but there was still lots of slurping, yelling and braying laughter interspersed with arguments. She winced as a tearing noise ended one pain-filled squeal and pitied the small warren of hares destroyed by the three vampiric Redcaps in their orgy of blood and body parts.

Mak shifted beside her in the gathering gloom. "They always like this?"

Cherith shuddered. "Yes. They're bloodthirsty, cunning and vicious and they'll attack without provocation."

"Vantark! Malkurk! Going!" A snarly response, the sound of swishing meadow grass, then feet slapping on rock.

Mak stirred. "They're on their way."

"To hunt for a Seelie Fae and a water girl."

A deep breath. "You know Cherith, that sounds an awful lot like *us*."

She swallowed. "Yes, they must've seen us."

"They referred to a River King. Exactly how many are there?"

"Every major river has one, b-but I thought there was only one in these parts, because there's only the Mirkdowd."

"So, you're working for the Mirkdowd River King – watching me – and they're hunting both of us. How's that make sense?"

"By the River Goddess, Mak, I don't know! Something weird is going on. We've never been asked to spy on anyone before you." She jerked their linked wrists. "What are you involved in?"

"Me? You think this is my fault?" Mak returned the yank. "I was simply looking for information about my ancestry. Then that thrice-damned Nageen wrecked everything."

"What's happening, then?"

"Better to ask why your River King's consorting with Redcaps
– that normal?"

"Quicksand no! Redcaps have no allies!"

"That's not what it sounds like."

Cherith threw up her hands, dragging Mak's with it. "I don't
understand!"

Mak yanked their joined arms down. "Can you not do that? It's
distracting and annoying."

She pinched the bridge of her nose. "Sorry."

He sighed. "Me too. Neither of us has the answer, plus it's dark
and we're up on a cliff."

"Oh for Goddess' sake, just fly us down to the meadow!"

"My pleasure!"

Mak's boots scraped on rock, his free arm encircling her, grip
firm. "Mmff!" When he leapt from the clifftop, Cherith turned her
face into his shoulder, stifling her scream of surprise, before
hastily winding her free arm around his strong neck. She barely
had time to enjoy the musky male scent of him before they landed.

"Not keen to go near the trees after the Redcap massacre, plus
the quicker we get what we came for and leave, the better." Mak
grimaced. "This hidden valley is a trap. How soon can we can look
for the flowers – are they hard to find?"

Cherith laughed. "This whole place is a mass of them. See those
tiny white star-shaped blossoms? They're glowing, even hidden
amongst all of the grass." She poked at the grass with her toes, her
foot separating blades to expose a glowing flower. "See?" Little
white dots glimmered in the gathering dusk.

"Huh. How many do we need?"

"I'm not sure." Cherith sighed. "Just pick some."

"A pity we don't have my backpack to hold them in."

"Well, we don't. Pockets will have to do."

Kneeling, Cherith parted more grass to show Mak the boun-
tiful presence of the star-shaped blooms. His every movement
disturbed the grass, revealing more flowers, releasing a delicate
perfume.

"I love the scent." Cherith drew deep breaths, noticing Mak's glance straying to her chest before he guiltily averted his eyes. *Damn it. He looks just as attracted to me as I am to him, or maybe I'm just the nearest female. I must remember this is a temporary glitch in our lives, not a permanent mating.*

"I SMELL THEM! THEY UP CLIFF!"

Cherith froze. Beside her, Mak jerked his head to look through the darkness towards the distant shout.

"River Goddess! I didn't think of scent!" Cherith scrambled to her feet and shrank into Mak. Drawing her close, he dropped a fast kiss on her cheek before releasing her. "We got this, Cherith. Remember the Nageen?"

Cheek tingling, she swallowed. "Can you fly us out of here?"

"It's too dark – I'd need moonlight at least; the area is unfamiliar."

"Okay. Let's go closer to the paving. Maybe we can get that cliff behind us?"

"Show me."

"This way!" Cherith lurched into a run, Mak sprinting beside her.

"THERE!"

"SEE THEM!"

The noise of talons tearing the sod was loud behind them. "Stop." Mak pulled up, forcing Cherith to comply. "There's not enough time to reach the cliff. We've got to face them."

Turning, Cherith stood tall beside Mak, bringing her hands up in readiness. Mak roared, spitting flame. The night lit up, blue-green phosphorescence soaring high to reveal three Redcaps galloping closer, their gait a peculiar sideways crablike stance, chunks of dirt flying out behind them as they ran. Fangs and jaw-tusks gleaming in the glow of the rising firebolt, the creatures jerked to a startled halt, milling uncertainly.

"Dracon!" A furious but fearful hiss. The light winked out.

"Fire gone now."

"Yay but where is it, eh? Dracon?"

"See only water girl and Seelie male."

"You! Water girl! Where Dracon?"

Cherith panted. "How badly do you wish to know, Redcap? Want an introduction?"

The only response to her taunt was some muttering. "If Dracon, we burn, Vantark."

"Bah! There no Dracons! She whelped by Eldwytch mage, Malkurx- she have evil fire potion."

"May have more fire potion ... careful."

The creatures bounded forward again.

"Now!" Mak barked.

"On it!" Instinctively, Cherith magically pushed water at the attacking goblins while Mak's new burst of flame coloured the night. She had no time to wallow in relief as their powers combined, the flame shading from jade green into aqua, then seafoam.

"Again! Keep going!"

Cherith kept pushing water in partnership to Mak's fiery blasts until her arms ached and her breath shuddered and gasped. Finally, Mak folded his fingers around hers and squeezed.

"Okay, we can stop." The night became dark and silent.

"They're done for?" Cherith sagged.

"NOT!" The guttural snarl came from behind them. A sudden heavy weight knocked them sprawling. Cherith hit the ground on her side, the impact making her dizzy. Beside her, Mak swore viciously. He reared to his knees but a blow flattened him again. "Down Seelie! River King say 'alive' but you let go Malkurx and Vantark or I—"

A brilliant golden firestorm blazed through the ether, cutting off the Redcap's growl. It left behind the nasty smell of burnt flesh. "You'll do nothing, Redcap scum."

At the sound of that voice, Mak stiffened, then grabbed Cherith tight, rolling as if the pair of them were a single entity.

"Old Venny?"

"You have a death wish, youngling? Letting the enemy outflank you?"

Cherith's mouth dropped open as she stared up into the black eyes of Old Venny the tinker trader, balancing a curl of golden flame on the palm of his hand.

CHAPTER ELEVEN

DEMAKSIM

"The Redcaps have night vision, Venny." Recovering from the attack, DeMaksim raised himself to a sitting position and helped Cherith up. "I don't. What in hell are you doing here? Not that I'm ungrateful, but there can't be much call for a tinker trader up here ... unless you trade with the Redcaps?"

"I'm passing through; luckily, for the pair of you." Old Venny sighed. "I'm guessing you've basic warrior training but no field experience?"

DeMaksim nodded. "Correct, the Fae Wars were well over before my coming of age." Drawing his legs up, he wrapped his free arm around his shins. "Once we realised the Redcaps were attacking, we made for the cliff, thinking to have it at our backs, but their speed forced us to make a stand. How'd you produce the flame?" The yellow fire was gone now.

"A new gadget I'm trying out." Venny looked away, rubbing his brow. "Those Redcaps are wily devils, for sure." He cocked his head. "Greetings Cherith Beriaden, it's been a while. What brought the pair of you here?"

"Hi Venny." Cherith waved. "We're harvesting antigeen flowers for a potion."

He grunted. "Plenty of those here. Which one of you crafts potions?" Old Venny's eyes flickered between them.

"Neither of us." DeMaksim grimaced. "We planned on asking Cherith's father to make the brew."

Old Venny raised an eyebrow. "Correct me if I'm wrong, but when we met up at Castle Synternesse, I understood you intended being home for All Hallows' Eve? That's one day away. If you're going to visit Cherith's father at the Beriaden home, you won't make your family's celebration."

DeMaksim frowned. "Things have changed."

"What things?"

"This, for one." DeMaksim raised his right hand, linked to Cherith's left.

Old Venny stepped closer. "A Nageen mating string?" He scratched his head. "How in the name of prime darkness did you manage to be trapped by that?"

DeMaksim flipped a hand. "I rejected her overtures, but she wouldn't accept that and—"

"Who, Cherith?" Old Venny's head tilted.

DeMaksim glowered. "No, the Nageen!"

"So how did Cherith become part of the scenario?"

"When I discovered her spying on me, we ended up in a struggle. The Nageen dropped from a tree and threw these red ropes at us—"

"I was not spying, Mak!"

"You're the one who answered your River King's call to watch me – that's spying isn't it?"

"No! That's doing my duty. But it's gone sour because now he's chasing both of us!"

Old Venny laughed. "Oh you younglings. Whilst your antics are extremely entertaining, can we stick to the tale? What about the Nageen?"

Cherith and DeMaksim exchanged glances. Cherith swallowed. "Ah, we sort of, um …"

"We killed her." DeMaksim's voice was flat.

Old Venny stared, his gaze shifting from one to the other. "Hmm." One eyebrow rose. "How?"

DeMaksim jerked a thumb over his shoulder. "Like that."

Raising his head, Old Venny eyed the looming lumps of Redcap stillness and pursed his lips. "I think I'd like a closer look." He sauntered off, returning a few minutes later. "Did you have to fight on my doorstep? Now I've got two solid green Redcap statues in my garden. Cyn will not be happy."

As Cherith and DeMaksim stared at him with equally puzzled looks, a female voice spoke.

"What won't I like, Ven, sweetie?"

"Our new lawn ornaments, Cyn darling." Old Venny kissed the lovely Lepidopter-fae female firmly. "Cyn, let me introduce you to DeMaksim Aphiski, and his partner, Cherith Beriaden. DeMaksim, Cherith, meet my mate Cynamelle."

Old Venny's mate was tall and slender with plum-coloured curls, blue eyes, Swallowtail butterfly wings and a wide smile. She wore a fitted violet tunic over black trousers with ankle boots of a deeper purple. "Pleased to meet you both." Cynamelle's voice was a pleasant contralto.

Old Venny grimaced. "You might change your mind when you see the gift they've provided."

"Gift?"

He pointed at the new statues. "Take a look, my dear." Cynamelle walked towards the Redcaps, a light blooming as she approached them.

"That's odd." Cherith frowned. "Did she have a candle or something, with her?"

"Or something."

The dryness of his tone drew DeMaksim's gaze. Old Venny stared back, eyes glimmering, taking DeMaksim's captive. He spun into dizzy blackness, adrift in bottomless wells of intense, expanding dark liquid, swirling down to a sea of darkness that went on and on, like a night without end. *Got to break his hold!* Lips firming, DeMaksim wrenched his gaze away, found himself panting. *Were those stars in his gaze?* Cautiously he checked. Old Venny grinned, his expression innocent, harmless; simply the old tinker trader DeMaksim had always known. *Did I imagine that?*

"Well, frozen green goblins certainly make a fancy decoration in our meadow." Cynamelle strolled up to her mate and drew his arm around her middle. "How did they end up like that?"

Old Venny snugged her tight, kissing her cheek. "My very next question. You read my mind, darling."

DeMaksim exchanged glances with Cherith.

"Which of you is responsible?" The tinker rubbed his chin. "Neither the Cherith nor DeMaksim I've visited over the years had that kind of power. Where'd it come from?"

DeMaksim wondered if he knew Old Venny the tinker trader as well as he'd thought. The whirlpool eyes had shaken him. He focused on Cherith. "What do you think?"

She gulped, grasping his fingers. "We're in over our heads, Mak – we need help and we'd be idiots to trust River King Eskavon now. Just tell them."

"Okay." DeMaksim shrugged. "Truth is, Cherith and I are both culpable."

"Hmm." Old Venny considered them. "Would you like to expand on that?"

"I told you I was searching for links to ancestors when we met at Castle Synternesse."

"For your family's All Hallows Eve ritual." Old Venny nodded.

"Well, there's more to the story. I'm actually looking for possible draconic ancestry."

Old Venny's eyebrows rose. "Which explains why you wanted the old scroll about Dracons translated. But what makes you think your family has draconic ancestry?"

"Maman." DeMaksim revealed. "She's a Neptulidae and because some of us manifested a power or ability appearing to have a draconic link, she believes someone in her family mated a Dracon. For instance, Zhulija can manifest heat and use it to power the forge in her art studio without being heat-affected in any way. She blows glass and works in metal."

"So, you're doing this research on her behalf?"

"No. I'm doing it for me." DeMaksim explained how his ability to bring on a few scales had, over the years, grown into producing a set of claws, some smoke from his nostrils, a lick of fire, then bursts of flame. "I felt out of control, needed answers, that's how it began. The translated scroll mentioned the Dark Reaches, so when we parted company, I headed here. Unfortunately, between swamp and thorny thickets, it's hard to find ground level entries. I flew some of the time, but once I'd entered the region, I wasn't sure where to go and didn't want to miss any clues; there's more people to talk to at ground level."

Cherith's fingers twitched in his. "Which is how you drew the attention of the River King and I was recruited by Aquinal the Nixie."

"And because of that, you're tied to me." DeMaksim snorted. "How's that for irony? Anyway, my first night I went to The Elderoak Inn."

"A pleasant hostelry." Old Venny stroked his chin again.

"That's where I met the Nageen." DeMaksim detailed the encounter, moved on to his morning introduction to Cherith and the Nageen's subsequent intrusive attack, causing DeMaksim and Cherith to defend themselves, culminating in the serpent-woman's death.

"Your flame altered from red to green and your powers combined with Cherith's to become hot frozen ice?" Old Venny frowned.

"Yes. After the Nageen wrapped us together in her mating string, those things changed."

The tinker's gimlet gaze pinned him. "That all?"

"No-o." DeMaksim spoke about their quest to come harvest the antigeens for a potion, Cherith's power taking on a new healing aspect, his fall into the river and inadvertent change into a Dracon with water characteristics. "From which I couldn't change back to a person."

"Fascinating." Cynamelle tapped her lip. "So, you're thinking a potion designed to combat Nageen venom will work on the binding?"

"Yes." Cherith sighed. "We're not really mates; all the changes come back to the Nageen linking cord. When that's gone, things will revert to normal."

"Hmm." Old Venny turned to look at them squarely. "Did either of you, at any stage since being bound together by the Nageen, exchange blood?"

"Ah, yes, we both did." DeMaksim glanced at Cherith, who nodded. "Is that why my draconic abilities surged and changed colour?"

"Partly." Old Venny's smile was mirthless. "This is where I need to remind you, that of the several events involved in a mating, one of the most important is a blood exchange."

DeMaksim choked.

Cherith's voice was a whisper. "W-what are you saying?"

Old Venny's mouth pursed. "I don't think the Nageen's binding matters."

"We're mated?" DeMaksim and Cherith were a single voice.

"Yes."

CHAPTER TWELVE

CHERITH AND DEMAKSIM

"*That's* ridiculous!" Cherith wasn't sure whether she felt elated, terrified or both. *How can Mak and I possibly be mated? Why did we exchange blood? So stupid, when we both know what it can do. Now, we might be stuck with each other.* She checked herself. *'Stuck' with him? Is that what I think?* A surge of emotion flooded her body; a definitive 'no'. She might have known Mak for only a couple of days, but he'd shown himself to be everything she desired in a mate. Suddenly, she wanted Old Venny to be right: she wanted to be Mak's mate. *But was that fair to him? Would he feel trapped? I couldn't deal with that, so when the time comes, I'll have to let him go.* Cherith tightened her lips, overwhelming sadness pushing out every other thought.

"Why is it ridiculous?" The tinker cocked his head, watching her.

She swallowed. "Blood is important, but it's not the only thing. People choose each other." She glanced from Old Venny to Cyn, on to Mak, found them all staring at her. Old Venny and Cyn shook their heads.

"Not in a true mating." Cyn's voice gentled. "That's a Goddess planned pairing. No rhyme, no reason and no returns."

"Ggllk?" Mak coughed. "You mean ... you're saying ... we ... this is a true mating?"

Old Venny nodded. "People can fall in love and choose to be mates, of course. They go through the same set of rituals as true mates, but without the same results. The easiest way to confirm true matings are by the changes the couple undergo. Only true mates take on new characteristics, develop new powers after their mating."

"But I already had draconic traits!"

"Which changed and increased."

"Well, what about Cherith? Nothing's changed for her." Mak's vazel eyes impaled her. "Has it?"

Throat dry, Cherith stared back, uncertain what answer he wanted. "Um."

"You said Cherith's green powers developed a new healing aspect. Your powers combined and changed to kill the Nageen." The tinker was relentless. "A Nageen's mating string binds a mate to *her*. The fact that she miscalculated and bound the two of you *together* has no relevance to the changes you've both experienced; they'd have happened anyway."

Cyn stirred. "Cherith, may I ask when you were last immersed in water?"

"Immersed?" Cherith struggled to think. "Well, we walked in the river, but full immersion hasn't happened since ... since Mak and I wrestled, then fought with the Nageen." Her hands flew to her cheeks. "Oh! Two days – I must be a wrinkled old hag!"

"Your skin looks as fresh and dewy as if you'd just left the water." Old Venny smiled. "Isn't that interesting?"

Cherith sagged. Mak's fingers tightened around hers. She winced at his frown; her voice emerged a whisper. "I'm sorry, I know you don't want this."

His frown deepened. "Don't be upset, we'll work it out."

She fought back tears. "What now?"

Cyn held out a hand, her smile inviting. "Now, I think you

should both come home with Venny and I. We'll have hot drinks and a meal, yeah?"

Mak nodded. "Okay, although I'm not sure where you're hiding your home. This place is all meadow, cliffs and trees." Standing, he held his other hand out to assist Cherith. She accepted the offer, making it a double handed effort. Pulling her close, Mak hugged Cherith with his free arm and rocked her gently.

"What happened to 'passing through'?" Mak's glare was dagger sharp.

"Well, we are. We're passing through our home, resting between trips; still counts as passing through." Old Venny grinned. "Watch your step, the paving is our front path."

Cherith hesitated. "But, there's only grass and a rock wall after the paving."

"Been up here before, have you?"

"Yes. I explore everywhere along the river looking for plants. It's how I knew where to find antigeen blossoms."

He chortled. "Appearances can be deceiving."

"If you say so." Following Cyn and Old Venny, Cherith wondered if the elderly male was losing his wits. She heard him mutter something as he and Cyn stepped off the paving stones, then, between one step and the next, disappeared.

Mak halted abruptly. "Blue blazes! Where'd they go?" Cherith hovered uncertainly beside him, but as they goggled, the tinker's head reappeared.

"Come on! What's taking so long?"

"Um, I don't think—"

"Good. Don't think, just follow." Old Venny winked, vanishing again.

Cherith shook her head. "Who, or what, is he?"

"Only one way to find out." Mak stepped forward determinedly, Cherith alongside.

DeMaksim stumbled into a foggy bottomless whirlpool with no up or down, left or right. He rotated in a disorienting haze with flickers and gouts of incandescent flame bursting spasmodically through the heavy mist. It reminded him of his fall from the willow's branch into the river. No breath, a huge weighted band constricting his lungs. Was he drowning? But there was no water; only vapour and fire.

The fog thinned. Flames surged around him, a writhing mass of colour, fluctuating back and forth across the spectrum. Gut churning, DeMaksim's dread escalated as the curling licks of fire crept closer, bursts of flame reaching amorphous fingers until the enormous conflagration engulfed him in a whoosh of heat and sensation. Someone screamed into the roar of the firestorm. He was burning, his whole body flaring like a torch. His vision tunnelled to a pinpoint of scorching red, then exploded into an inferno of green and blue. He spun in a sense-deprived, flaming mass of bewildered panic and breathlessness, wondering how a quest for an ancestor had become a monstrous nightmare certain to take his life.

Gasping and struggling, his thoughts flew to Cherith. Her hand had been tucked into his; she was tied to him and in equal danger. *I've got to save her!* Concentrating hard, forcing himself to ignore the holocaust, DeMaksim sought the internal link he'd forged with Cherith when she treated the willow.

It wasn't there. For a moment, he doubted, then his resolve firmed.

If we linked like that once, we can do it again! He redoubled his efforts, ignoring the spasming of his muscles, enduring the fiery external hell. His reward was the sound of his own heartbeat, beating in a crazy rhythm. The beats needed to be smoother, more regulated. As he thought it, imagining the beats as they should be, so they were.

His confidence rose. *I can do this! I know she's next to me.* Pushing seeking energy out from his heart, across his chest, down his right arm and through to his fingers, he found other fingers grasped within them. *Cherith!* Carefully, he threaded his awareness into her body, determined she'd not be sacrificed along with him. She must live.

Now that he knew the way of it, he forged a link with Cherith's mind in next to no time. *Cherith!*

Mak?

Yes, I've got to save you!

You must control the fire, Mak! Control the fire!

What?

But that reminder of the external blaze snapped his concentration and he lost his link to her. Around him, flames of red and aqua fought for supremacy, a wicked inferno. *Control this? How? I know I control flame as a Dracon, but this is ...* Awareness bloomed. His draconic flame had been red until he and Cherith combined. After that it had become greenish blue. He was surrounded by his own flame?

Opening his mouth, he roared, sucking in air. The flames wavered slightly, surging as he paused. *Oh no, you don't!* Rounding his lips, he inhaled, then inhaled again, siphoning the flame. It eased towards him, drawn into his mouth on the next inhale. He swallowed it, drew more inside, kept swallowing, grabbed handfuls of the stuff and fed it to himself, swallowing until the last lick of aqua fire disappeared inside his mouth. Sealing his lips, throat working, he massaged his stomach, burped massively. Gravity surged into him and he fell, landing supine on a fluffy surface.

Daze receding, DeMaksim became aware of weight on his chest. Opening one eye, he peered down – met Cherith's anxious gaze as she lay half on and half off him. He conjured a weak smile. Another figure loomed. Squinting, he identified Old Venny.

Voice croaking, he addressed the elderly tinker trader. "What in blue blazes happened?"

"Well done, youngling." Old Venny smiled. "Welcome to our home. Cyn's getting you a cool drink."

"But, that fire? That's your normal doorway?" DeMaksim's bewildered gaze moved to Cherith. "You survived it too?"

"I didn't experience the same thing." Cherith's usual soft apricot complexion looked pale. "It was terrifying seeing you as a ball of flame, but Old Venny said you had to merge your two personalities and gain control of them."

"Wait a minute." DeMaksim glared at Old Venny, hands curling into fists. "You knew that would happen?"

The older man nodded, his expression wary. "Yes, I bespelled the portal."

Cherith tilted her head. "Why do you need a portal into your home?"

"Our home is on a separate plane of reality. The portal is how Cyn and I access it. We—"

"You magicked the portal against us and didn't give any warning?" Cherith's shaking fingers wormed their way inside his fist.

Old Venny ran a hand through his mane of silvery black hair. "Warning you would reduce the effectiveness; you had to work out the answers and find the control."

"You know that, how?" A growl edged DeMaksim's voice.

"You're not the first draconic fledgling I've dealt with." Old Venny's eyes were fathomless.

"Draconic fledgling? I worked through something completely outside the realms of probability and understanding, putting Cherith at risk and you not only *knew*, you set it up?" DeMaksim crouched, eyeballing Old Venny.

The older male tensed. "The magic was specific. Cherith was never in danger."

Roaring, an explosion of rage eclipsing reason, DeMaksim hissed a gout of aqua flame at Old Venny. Eyes flashing, the tinker's return blast of golden flame met the aqua head on; a flaring wall of power. The clash burst in a spiralling wheel of gold and aqua sparks, before the gold swallowed the aqua and the fire vanished in a thunderous shock-wave that swept the room.

Mouth dry, DeMaksim stared. "Wha—?"

Cherith simply gaped.

Luckily the room they occupied was large, because, crouched

in front of them, head snaked forward, was a large black Dracon, bared fangs glistening. His smouldering voice rang with warning. "Pull yourself together youngling, I've no wish to hurt you. Don't force it on me."

DeMaksim's mouth dropped; his rage died as he stared at the looming figure. "You? You're a Dracon! How's that possible?"

A hooting buzz of laughter answered. "Haven't figured it out yet, youngling? *I'm* your draconic ancestor. Say hello to Great Grandpa Venstilarquon."

CHAPTER THIRTEEN

CHERITH

"*N*ow that the theatrics are over, here's the promised drink. It's hot chocolate." Cyn's tray held four steaming mugs. "Venny darling, give him a chance to find calm."

Cherith clasped her mug firmly, observing the two males. Old Venny, having shrugged off his draconic form, had assisted a shell shocked Mak to a large cushion-strewn, wooden pew. Cherith plopped beside him, equally grateful to sit. Their transition from the meadow into grey foggy nothingness before exiting the portal into Cyn and Venny's home, had sent her nerves into quivering overdrive. Seeing Mak beside her as a flaming torch, one which ceased at their link, had left her speechless with terror. She still wasn't certain she could speak.

Mak massaged his forehead. "Could you please explain what you meant when you told Cherith I had two selves?"

"Sure." Old Venny sipped from his mug, sparing his mate a glance. "Thanks, Cyn. This is perfect." He eyed Cherith and Mak. "Your description of a full draconic change after the river dunking, your inability to make the change back and the fact the necessary change happened by accident while you slept, told me your two inner entities weren't melded."

Mak frowned. "You mean I'm a split personality?"

"In a way." Old Venny licked chocolate from his lip. "A shapeshifter is one person with two aspects, but they're still, essentially, one being. Whilst some fledglings develop the skill of unification instinctively, others require instruction – which isn't a problem if you grow up within a family of shapeshifters."

"But I didn't." Mak crossed his legs at the ankle. "So how do I combine the two parts of myself?"

Old Venny waved a hand. "You've done it; that's what the spell was about. I rigged the entry portal to force the issue."

Mak shook his head. "You realise that Cherith and I could have been burned or worse with all of that fire contained in the portal?"

The older Dracon snorted. "Hardly. It was your flame, which can't harm either you, or your mate." Old Venny raised his hand, forestalling Mak's next heated outburst. "Enough – we've covered this. You mastered the flame wearing your Fae-male body as you had to; that's sufficient to trigger the changes to align both your aspects."

Mak glared. "Fine. Thanks, I think." He cocked his head. "Except, it's not fine. Why, if you suspected all this, didn't you say something when I saw you at Castle Synternesse? Why put me through all this? I thought something was truly wrong with me."

"I'm sorry for that, but Dracons retreated from sight for a reason. Usually interlopers are discouraged and I couldn't be certain how much of the Dracon existed in your line even though I knew you to be a descendant." Old Venny took another mouthful from his mug. "That's why I dropped clues to bring you to the Dark Reaches without straightforward directions. If you were determined enough to find your way into the territory and subsequently, to me, I'd discover why. Which I have. Although, if I'd known it was because you were developing draconically, I'd have been more forthcoming. I watch for that trait in our descendants; I've never seen it in you during any of my visits. How long has it been occurring?"

Mak cradled his mug. "Years. When flame happened, there

were times it scared the Fae-lights out of me and I knew I needed help." He sighed. "Turning full Dracon has only eventuated since meeting Cherith." He sipped his drink, gaze going to Cyn. "So, Old Venny is related to me, but how are you connected to all this?"

Cyn's spoon clinked in her mug. "Here's where I confess that I'm Cynamelle Neptulidae." Her expression challenged as she met Mak's blank stare, but she smiled as he clicked his fingers.

"The 'Mel' family connection I was looking for!"

"Yes." Her smile morphed into a laugh. "Venny and I confused the records on purpose, to disguise my identity and make it harder to locate anyone draconic, or draconically connected. Secrecy is as much a part of my life as it is my mate's when it comes to safe-guarding Draconfolk. Good to know we were so successful."

Cherith propped her elbow on the arm of their seat, resting her chin on her hand. "May I ask why?"

"A number of reasons." Replacing his mug on the tray, the elder Dracon laced his fingers together. "Some personal, some draconic – most I'm not at liberty to share. Suffice to say, we Dracons deemed it wise; many of us don't play well with others. However, I'm not the only one with descendants – we watch for those who need help. It's one of the reasons I travel as a tinker trader, as do a few others of my kind."

"You're sure I'm okay? That I'll be able to manage my draconic nature? How much experience have you had?" Mak leaned forward. "I mean—" He stared. The Dracon and his mate were laughing uproariously. "What's the joke?"

Old Venny gasped, wiping his eyes. "The joke's more on me, young Mak. You need to consult your copy of the old scroll and study the names on it. Then ask me how much experience I've had."

"Er, you knew I made a copy?"

A wry twist wrinkled Old Venny's lips. "It's what I'd have done."

Mak closed his eyes briefly. "A-and you're on it?"

A nod as Old Venny leaned back and crossed his hands behind his head. "Oh, yes."

"Then you're a Primordial."

"So, how old am I, youngling?"

Mak swallowed. "A-as old as the world."

"Older. I saw this world birthed." Old Venny's voice softened. "I watched the other Dracon Primordials coalesce from the magical ether of creation. As for me, I'm a breath of space dust, a child of the stars, I'm *The* Primordial."

"By the Great Goddess." Cherith whispered incredulously. "You've probably forgotten more than we'll ever know."

Galaxies wheeled and burned in the fathomless black eyes focused on Cherith. She shivered. He wasn't simply Old Venny or Venstilarquon; he was *the* Venstilarquon, the ultimate Primordial. "I forget nothing."

Mak's expression was awestruck. "Blue blazes, your brain must be a seething morass!"

A dry chuckle heralded Old Venny's return. "Nah. I've just got amazing storage capacity up here." Tapping his skull, he drew laughter and eased tension. He speared Mak with a look. "You and I need to spend time together, grandson. There are things you must learn. First we'll need to free the pair of you from the clutches of a failed Nageen mating." His gaze shifted to Cherith. "We'll collect the antigeen blossoms and be on our way at dawn. Will Istondir be at home?"

Cherith tongued chocolate on her mug's rim. "Yes. Cassie has gone home to make sure."

Old Venny pursed his mouth. "We'll save time and fly."

"Flying?" Cherith winced.

Amusement curled the corners of the Dracon's lips. "That *is* what wings do."

"I'm not keen." Cherith bit her lip. "Apart from when he was stuck as a Dracon, Mak and I mostly walked."

"Walking from here to your family cottage?" Old Venny studied her. "I thought you wanted to be free of the Nageen's binding?"

"I do." Cherith rolled her bottom lip between her teeth.

"I don't blame you for drawing the captivity out; Mak is rather

88

gorgeous." Cyn winked. "Reminds me of Old Venny when he chooses not to show his age."

"No! That's not ... I mean ..."

Cyn's eyebrows rose. "You don't think Mak is handsome?"

"Yes, of course he is. Oh, gah!" Cheeks burning, Cherith subsided against the cushions. The sofa padding depressed as Mak leaned in.

"Cyn's teasing, but it *would* save lots of time if you agreed to fly. I kept you safe last time, remember?" Cherith did. She'd enjoyed it too, but was still having qualms over thoughts of repeating the experience.

She peeped at him. "Can we re-visit the idea in the morning?"

Mak nodded. "If that's what you need."

Muttering, Old Venny rolled his eyes. Cyn pointed a stern finger at him, but her lips quivered.

He threw up his hands. "Fine, we'll sleep on it."

"Come along Cherith, Mak." Cyn stood. "I'll show you to your bedroom."

Old Venny's grumbling was low-voiced but audible. "Afraid to fly? I don't understand. It's not like she's a fish out of water, or anything. Why, flying is as natural as breathing!"

"Sarcasm is the lowest form of wit." Cherith glowered as she sidled past him. "Try repeating your comment when Maman can hear you."

"Or not." Old Venny grimaced. "Your mother's never afraid to fight." He eyed her. "You're clearly not a chip off the maternal block where that's concerned."

"Venny!" Cyn's hands were on her hips.

Stopping so suddenly that Mak crashed into her, Cherith shook her head. "You misunderstand, *Gramps.* I'm refraining in consideration to your extreme age – I wouldn't want to hurt a doddering old person. Maman won't give two hoots for any of that. Can't wait to see you get your comeuppance at the hands of a fish-lady."

Mak's arm encircled her waist as he laughed in open delight. "Oh, good one Cherith."

"Why you cheeky youngster!"

Cherith echoed Cyn's earlier action, pointing at Old Venny. "And that's another thing – you need an attitude adjustment. Calling Mak a youngling, or a fledgling and labelling me a youngster, is demeaning. We may have plenty to learn and be a lot younger than you, but we're still adults. We deserve to be treated as such, so sleep on that too, Gramps."

CHAPTER FOURTEEN

DEMAKSIM

*M*orning sun peeped around the curtains, birds twittering as they went about their business. DeMaksim wondered at the reality of those things; his observations the previous evening made him think the home of Cyn and Old Venny was a massive, made-over cave, its high ceilings catering for a Fae-male who was sometimes a Dracon. Or was that a Dracon who masqueraded as a Fae-male? Old Venny said the home was not on a normal plane of reality, so where'd the windows with sunlight and birds come from?

He could slide out of bed and open the curtains to see, but DeMaksim was loath to move. Cherith was snuggled up, half on and half off his body as she'd been when they camped on the river islet, and he was enjoying her proximity. Unable, and unwilling, to sleep, he pondered their last few days. Here in the Dark Reaches, he'd become Mak: adventurer, historian, Dracon … mate. It felt real, not as if he was hanging around to fill a father-shaped hole if Yanvian Aphiski, the current Duke of Papillion, should die—immortality didn't guarantee you couldn't be killed after all. The Fae Wars 50 years ago were the most recent proof of that. Seelie versus Unseelie. Something he'd never understood. They were all Fae, both variants of the same magical race. His side, the Seelie, were supposed to be honourable, moral and good; on the side of Light. Did it follow then that the Unseelie were dishonourable, immoral, bad and on the side of Dark?

What did that even mean? He'd met Seelie Fae whose honour and morals were heavily tarnished. His youngest sister, Zhulija had met, been courted by, and was now mated to, Dario Eribifax, known as The Unseelie Beast. Dario had shown them strong morals and a high degree of honour – nothing about him was remotely 'bad'. Not in the terms DeMaksim knew.

Now DeMaksim's mate was an Unseelie Undine-Eldwytch – and she was wonderful. Recalling events since meeting Cherith, he agreed with his multitude of greats-Grandpa. Looking down at Cherith's sweet face filled him with a feeling of home; she'd very quickly become his centre, his life goal, his reason for being. Yep, the adorable female in his arms was is true mate. All their physical changes proved it – despite Cherith being Unseelie Fae. Another who didn't fit the immoral, dishonourable and/or bad label. Conclusion? The definition he'd learned and believed in his entire life was wrong. So, what was the real meaning of the gulf between the Seelie and the Unseelie? They were definitely a sundered race. Why? Did Old Venny know?

Ignoring that, he and Cherith were physically tied together in a connection which should've disintegrated when the Nageen died. The search to break the link between Cherith and himself had caused him to stray from his goals of finding answers to his personal physical changes and his draconic ancestry. Yet, the answers he'd been seeking had come to him anyway. He'd discovered who and what he was and he'd stumbled upon Old Venny – ancestors and expectations, who knew?

Head tucked under his chin, Cherith stirred, mumbling incoherently. He swallowed, waited as she sighed and squirmed. Her face scrunched, her head turned a fraction and she rubbed that cute nose against his chest. He'd be lying if he said he didn't enjoy every second of her wake-up; the action in his groin was a giveaway.

Cherith's eyelids lifted; aqua eyes regarded him, deep pools in a river of mystery. Who knew what was beneath the surface until they dived down and became hooked on snags concealed in the depths? All of the best catches lurked in the deeps; anyone who fished could tell you that. *I've been snared and I never knew how wonderful it would be.* The thought came out of nowhere, seizing him. He couldn't take his eyes off her. Not just his mate; he was in love.

"Mak." A tiny smile curled her mouth.

"Good morning, Cherith." He smiled back. They had the rest of their lives together – as soon as they rid themselves of the Nageen's binding. "We've got to get moving. Convey the antigeen blossoms to your father as quickly as possible. The tie is a complete nuisance we've got to dispose of so we can be free to live our lives."

Rubbing her eyes, Cherith ducked her head. When she raised it again, the smile was gone. "Freedom. Yes, absolutely. No time to waste. Today – no, tonight is All Hallows' Eve and you planned to be with your family. Let's get moving and give you a chance to get there – you could still make it if you fly in your Dracon form." She sounded cheerful.

As they eased from the bed, poured water from the ewer into the basin and took turns washing, she continued to sound joyful. DeMaksim stood with his back to her, giving her privacy to wash as she chattered. She shared information about the plants and blossoms she nurtured, both up and down the river. She hummed. When it was his turn to wash and clean his clothes with a whisper of magic, she politely turned her back to him, her talk returning to his family and how he must miss them. DeMaksim couldn't get a word in, never mind talk about a shared future. She appeared driven, determined, unapproachable. He was left scratching his head.

Over pancakes with hot syrup and fresh berries, Cyn brought

up the concept of flying again. "It'd be much easier descending to river level, save a lot of time, Cherith. Would you reconsider? Tied to Mak as you are, you can't possibly fall."

Swallowing a mouthful, Cherith laid her spoon down. "I know I'm being squeamish, especially with Mak on a time-line."

Cyn wrinkled her nose. "Time-line?"

"He told his folks he'd return for their All Hallows' Eve celebrations." Old Venny spoke around a mouthful of pancake, his eyes flicking from Cherith to DeMaksim. "That won't happen."

Cherith glared. "It will if he flies. So I will fly."

"Excellent. But you'd have to go too." Another mouthful of syrupy pancake filled Old Venny's mouth.

"Not if we meet Papan and get the potion to rid us of these bonds." Cherith's hands covered her hips. "Anyway, Mak should take you, not me – you're the draconic ancestor."

DeMaksim, hand dragged along, prodded her hip, his voice crisp. "I'm not going home, so this argument is pointless."

Cherith's glare deepened. "My thoughts are not pointless!"

"No, they're not. I apologise." DeMaksim watched her. "If I was to take anyone, my choice would be *you*, okay? Now, are the flowers we picked last night still okay? Or do we need fresher blossoms?"

Mouth open, Cherith stared at him.

"Take both old and new." Cyn drew everyone's attention as she pointed from plate to plate and gestured; the plates stacked themselves. More gesturing moved the stack across the room to a distant workbench. "Some potions need fresh stuff and others are fine with dry."

"True." Cherith grinned. "Levitating dishes away – I like it." DeMaksim relaxed, pleased her ire had vanished.

Cyn laughed. "It's always been a good party trick." She beckoned her mate, who was rolling another pancake ready to eat. "Come on darling, eat that and let's get moving. I'd like to inspect my new lawn ornaments in daylight."

Everyone laughed. Old Venny chomped the pancake, swallowed and wiped his mouth with his napkin as he led the way across the room to the large rug below a niche in the cave wall.

DeMaksim frowned. "You're sure it's safe?"

Old Venny grinned. "Don't worry, the experience will be nothing like last time. Just follow Cyn and I. Here's a pack to put the fresh antigeens in. I've put last night's crop inside already, along with some food." Brows knitting, staring as if he could see right through the rock, Old Venny finally nodded. "It's safe outside. Let's go." Seconds later, he and Cyn vanished.

Despite feeling dubious, DeMaksim clasped Cherith's hand, grabbed the new pack and took the first step. They were immediately surrounded by white fog, but a pace later the sunny meadow materialized. DeMaksim squeezed Cherith's fingers gently. "Let's grab some fresher antigeens." As they picked the white blossoms, Cyn wandered over to the large frozen Redcap statues. She gave them a thorough inspection, her expression oddly delighted.

Old Venny approached as they finished. "Got the flowers? Good. Morph and let's get down to the river. Cherith can immerse herself as her Undine side needs." Cocking his head, he studied her. "Although, you still look as fresh as if you'd just left the water."

Cyn sauntered up, peering at Cherith. "How do you feel?"

"Fine." Cherith pursed her lips. "It's weird, but I feel as if I've recently been in water."

DeMaksim shrugged. "We'll play safe and stick to the plan. Stand back while I see if I can shift." Reconstructing his Dracon in his mind, he thought about becoming it. A tingle chased over him, the world blurred in sparkly mist and he was Dracon standing in the sunshine. Noticing Cherith dangling from his foreleg, he hastily cupped her in his other paw and helped her scoot astride his forearm.

She clutched him tightly. "Thanks."

"Good job." Old Venny's voice issued from the large draconic form taking up space nearby. He wore iridescent black scales, bat-like wings and, like DeMaksim, had three horns on his skull. "Told you things'd be fine."

Smoke plumed from DeMaksim's nostrils. "As long as I can change back."

Old Venny rolled his eyes. "Come on, Cyn." He crouched, extended a forepaw and helped her climb into place astride his neck.

"Hey." DeMaksim eyed Cyn. "You're Lepidopter-Fae – you're not using your wings?"

"My little ones against draconic wings?" She hooted. "You're crazy to think that'd work." Old Venny shook his head.

DeMaksim sighed. "Of course, never thought of that." Old Venny spread his wings, crouched low and launched into the air. DeMaksim dropped his gaze to Cherith. "You still okay with this?" She nodded, so he opened his wings and leapt skyward in pursuit of the black Dracon.

Gaining some height, he flew across the meadow, cleared the cliff and circled above the Mirkdowd River. Lower down, Old Venny and Cyn landed on the far bank. DeMaksim spiralled down to join them, touching down gently on the sandy shore.

Cherith peered at him. "Can you take me to the water?"

"Right." DeMaksim strode to the river, waded in, then sat, moving his foreleg closer to the water.

"Thanks, that's perfect." Cherith slid sideways into the current until she was submerged before floating to the surface. She scrunched water from her hair.

"With the mating changes, does it feel as good as it usually does … being in the water?"

"Yes." She sighed. "Even though I don't seem to need it as much as before, it's still nice. It's where I belong." She looked away, bit her lip, staring downstream. He wished he knew what she was thinking when she looked like that. He was about to ask when her gaze sharpened.

"What's that?"

"Company." Old Venny moved closer. "Saw them a few moments ago."

"Them, who?"

"Cascade and Beckett."

"What? Why?"

The elder Dracon raised eyebrows. "Looking for you, perhaps? They're your siblings. Unless you think they've ventured this far on a casual swimming expedition?"

DeMaksim fought to restrain laughter, but when Cyn chuckled, a snort of mirth escaped.

"Yeah, yeah, very funny." Cherith curled her lip. "But if Cassie and Becks are looking for me, it's because something's wrong."

CHAPTER FIFTEEN

CHERITH

"*Y*our brother and sister only speak to you when something's wrong?" Surprise permeated Mak's voice.

Cherith huffed a laugh. "No, I should have said important, not wrong."

Mak flexed his claws as Cherith's siblings approached. "What are they doing?"

Cassie and Becks had stopped a good distance away, Becks scowling, while Cassie hugged her Narwhal tusk dagger.

"Hmm." Cherith frowned. "I have no idea."

"It's the company you're keeping." Old Venny sat back on his haunches. "How harmless do you think we look, Mak?"

"Oh, yes, of course." Cherith nodded. Dracons were considered a myth and yet, here were two; no wonder Cassie and Becks maintained distance.

Becks cupped hands around his mouth and called, "Cherry? Everything okay?"

Cherith waved. "Yes, I'm with friends; it's safe to join us." Becks and Cassie swam slowly toward them, their eyes flickering to each person waiting in the shallows. Cherith surged forward as far as their linked limbs allowed. Mak, for his part, lowered his bulk in the water trying to appear smaller, less threatening.

Cherith and her siblings hugged, their smiles huge. "It's so good to see you both. But Cassie, weren't you supposed to be with Papan helping him prepare to make the potion?"

Cassie's smile dropped away like falling leaves. "Oh, Cherry! I didn't even get to tell Papan about the potion because River King Eskavon arrived and took Maman and Papan hostage. He wants to exchange them for you and Mak!" Her gold skin was cream-pale, her hands twisting constantly around the handle of her Narwhal tusk. "He said you're a traitor and you ran off with Mak. I told him about the crazy Nageen linking you together, but the only proof is a frozen statue, so he didn't believe me. He said he's never heard of anyone with power like that and—" Cassie tossed up her hands. "He's just crazy!"

"Becks?" Bewilderment rang in Cherith's voice.

"It's true." His lips firmed. "He arrived accompanied by a squad of Nixies."

"Headed by Aquinal." Cassie grimaced. "I can't imagine why that Nixie got mixed up in this."

Cherith glanced at her sister. "He's probably following orders, but that's irrelevant, right now."

Becks shot Cherith a grateful glance. "We left right away to find you and Mak."

"But Cherry!" Cassie clutched Cherith's arm. "Where *is* Mak? If we're to save Maman and Papan, we need him! Where is he? How did you get free? Are these Dracons? Is that Cyn, Old Venny the tinker trader's mate? Did the Dracons eat Old Venny and Mak?"

Rolling his eyes, Becks splashed his sister with water. "By Eletherion and the River Goddess, Cassie! Stop panicking and let these people speak. It's obvious that Cherry and Lady Cyn are completely unharmed and, by the way the black Dracon is laughing, I think it's safe to say you've invented a load of quicksand."

Cassie burst into tears. "I'm sorry!"

"Shh." Cherith hugged her as best she could with one arm and saw Becks staring over her shoulder. He studied the binding at her wrist, followed the link to Mak, his gaze rising up Mak's gleaming foreleg to the scaled and feathered head.

He stared hard at their wrist-foreleg proximity, then cocked an eyebrow. "Since you're attached to Cherry, I'm going to take a wild guess that you're Mak?"

"Correct." Mak extended his other foreleg. "Heir-Lord DeMaksim Yanvian Aphiski at your service, although, you can just call me Mak."

Becks tried to clasp Mak's paw in his hand, but could only manage a single claw. "A pleasure to meet you. I'm Junior Mage Beckett Mornenion Beriaden, known hereabouts as Becks." Eyes gleaming, Becks switched his gaze between Mak and Old Venny. "You two are really something amazing. Clearly, the report of the demise of Dracons is completely fabricated."

"Well, now that the secret's out ..." Old Venny waded forward, Cyn still perched around his neck. "I'm Venstilarquon. You already know my mate Cynamelle." Becks stiffened, peering at him, then up at Cyn and back. He did a double take, his mouth falling open.

"Old Venny?"

Behind Becks, Cassie choked, her hands flying to her cheeks. "You're *Old Venny*?"

"Been a while, Becks." The black Dracon winked.

"All this time ..." Becks shook his head. "By Eletherion, you *do* know how to keep a secret."

Old Venny's eyes rolled. "As you say. Now what's this nonsense about Eskavon?"

"Nonsense?"

Venstilarquon the Black snorted. "When you've been around as long as I have, you've seen a lot of supposedly intelligent people do some damned stupid things. Apparently Eskavon is proving my point."

"Well, this time his 'nonsense' involves my family." Becks looked towards Cherith and Mak.

Mak nodded. "Since the Seelie and Unseelie Fae are currently at peace under the combined rule of Queens Dianathke and Maerovana, this is senseless."

Cherith could only shake her head. "River King Eskavon, as Unseelie Fae, is subject to the joint Queens' rule – so what wasp's gotten into his trousers?"

"He's calling Mak a Queens' spy." Becks frowned.

Old Venny wrinkled his snout. "My hunch? He's not happy about Fae unity."

"Blue blazes." Mak swiped claws through the water, the corners of his mouth pinched. "Either he's gone mad or he's a rebel. Dario needs to know – keeping the Fae peace and locating rebels are within his jurisdiction."

"Dario?" Cassie licked her lips. "Are you referring to dreamy Lord Dario Eribifax, The Unseelie Beast?"

Mak's stare drilled into her. "I'm talking about Duke Dario Eribifax Garadenya, true mate to my sister, Zhulija."

"Oh, sorry, I meant no offense." Cassie's chagrin flushed her cheeks. "Sometimes news is slow to spread through the Dark Reaches." She smiled nervously. "A true mating, how lovely, and he's your brother-in-law? You must be thrilled."

Cherith sighed, ignoring Mak's chuckle. "Alright Cassie, stop now before plunging any deeper into the foot-in-mouth whirlpool you've created."

"There are bigger problems." Becks frowned at Cassie.

Cassie tucked hair behind an ear. "I know. We've got to free Maman and Papan without giving over Mak and Cherry. Not to mention that Papan can't make a potion from the antigeen flowers while he's a prisoner and if we trade Mak and Cherry to free Papan to make the potion, they won't be able to use the potion because they'll be prisoners instead. We don't want that to happen, because neither Cherry nor Mak have done anything wrong and, anyway, who'd want to be at the mercy of someone who's a madman or a criminal?" She flung her arms wide, smiling hopefully. "Right?" Her smile faltered when she caught everyone staring.

Becks shook his head. "Cassie, sometimes I really ... never mind. You're mostly right despite that confused rambling."

Old Venny tapped a claw against his jaw. "A paradox. We need to decide what we're going to do. Anyone got any ideas?"

Mak eyed Becks. "When the River King attended the arrest of your parents, did he give terms or instructions?"

Becks' mouth twisted. "His instructions were to meet at the Whortlebog, at dawn tomorrow for an exchange. If we don't comply within an hour of dawn, he said he'd kill Maman. If we haven't arrived by noon, he'll kill Papan too."

Cherith gasped.

A cloud of smoke issued from Old Venny's nostrils. "He's definitely crazy if he plans to kill both hostages when doing that will not only alienate his own people, but start a war with the Eldwytch."

"So, we've got about 18 hours." Mak hummed, thoughts churning. "How fast can we fly, Gramps?"

"Hmm." Old Venny's eyes narrowed. "It's only a couple of hours to reach Whortlebog, but that's not what you're asking, is it?"

"No. Is there enough time for you to reach Castle Synternesse, alert Queen Maerovana and maybe bring her and a couple of warriors back, while I fly home to collect Dario and Papan?"

Old Venny squinted. "That'd work."

Cassie glared, smacking the surface of the river with her palms. "What good will that do? You'll just be bringing a whole lot of important people here to watch my family die!"

Becks reached for her arm. "Think Cassie. They're also some of the most powerful people amongst the Fae and we'll have the element of surprise. Eskavon won't be expecting to confront Queen Maerovana or the Unseelie Beast – we might have a chance."

"Might?" Cassie flung her hands high.

Cherith scowled. "Do you have another plan, Cassie? Because, right now, nobody else does." Cassie covered her face with her hands, shaking her head.

Frown easing, Old Venny turned back to Mak. "If we leave straight away, we'll give our reinforcements time to make whatever preparations they require. It'll also give us a few hours to rest up before flying back." Old Venny squinted. "If you begin the return journey in the early hours of tomorrow morning, you'll be here early enough to further throw Eskavon off-balance by setting up at the Whortlebog first."

Cyn cleared her throat. "Venny, we should take Cassie and Becks back to our place for the tonight. There's no point us going to the Whortlebog early, and you'll be better able to concentrate if you know I'm safe."

"Excellent idea." Old Venny nodded. "Come on, you two, climb up behind Cyn and I'll drop the three of you off outside our door. Mak, you and Cherith get going."

"Wait, where will we meet?"

"Look for a draconically shaped rock in the forest not far from the Whortlebog. Be there at least an hour before dawn."

"Okay." Mak grinned. "Hey Becks, Cassie, watch out for that first step across the portal at Cyn and Venny's – it's nasty!"

Cyn gurgled a laugh.

Old Venny's mouth twisted. "Smart arse!"

CHAPTER SIXTEEN

DEMAKSIM

*H*ours later, DeMaksim spied the Rubiconia River, worked out exactly where he was along its meandering length and swung south to fly past Garadenya Island, now the Duchy of Garadenya. Banking to the right, he glanced down at Cherith. She was supine on his foreleg, arms and legs wrapped around him. Every time he'd checked, she was intent on the panorama below. He smiled wryly; huge progress from her previous fear of flying.

"You doing okay, Cherith?"

"Yes! Is that Garadenya Island? I thought that's where The Beast lived now." They'd not flown far when she'd astonished him by communicating with him via their minds, explaining that she'd followed the trail he'd blazed during his portal fight. It was the best way to talk when atmospheric winds, combined with flight speed, made verbal speech impossible. Another mating perk.

"It is, but we're going to the Papillion Duchy – I've realized they'll all be there preparing for tonight's All Hallows' Eve celebration and bonfire."

For the first time since their departure, she twisted her head to stare at him, eyes huge. *"Your home. With all your family."*

"That's right."

"But – all your family! And you're stuck to me! We've been forced into mating and—"

"I don't think that matters right now, does it?" It certainly didn't matter to him. Especially not since finding out they were true mates. Although, if he was truthful with himself, he hadn't even minded it before that either. But did Cherith? She seemed so focused on them being separated. In her mind were they simply tragically tied together by the mating strings of a now dead Nageen? His heart sank. Maybe she didn't want to accept the true mating.

Her head dropped to his paw. "What will your family think of me?"

"You're adorable – they'll love you." Just like he did. There wasn't any aspect of Cherith he didn't delight in. Considering there'd been no choice but to live in each other's pockets, that was saying something. He hoped she felt affection for him, at least.

The Papillion Estate hove into view. "There! That place with all the gardens, the fences and gates stretching along the river. The one with the huge house – that's the part of the estate we've cultivated to live on."

"River Goddess! That's your home? It's amazing. And massive. No wonder your Papan requires help to manage it."

"Estate management is the last thing on my mind right now." The wind whipped her laugh back to him as he dropped height and crossed the boundary.

BOOM!

Powerful force-waves catapulted them backwards across the sky. Cherith screamed as her body was tossed outward in a wide arc around their link point. Wings stretched agonisingly, DeMaksim bunched his muscles and fought his way out of a somersault to level out, heart in mouth as he saw Cherith dangling. "Cherith!"

Swinging her left leg over his foreleg, Cherith began climbing. DeMaksim reached with his other paw to help her. "I'm sorry, I forgot the make-up of the protective field. I thought it'd still know me, but *it mustn't have recognised my draconic form."* He banked to avoid the still looming boundary.

Her grip firmed. *"Or me at all."*

"I thought it'd be okay because you're with me – I'll land and change shape."

By the time he touched down outside the gates and morphed back to his Fae-male form, the entrance was swamped by a crowd, with the guards trying to organise some semblance of control.

"They probably heard the explosion leagues away." DeMaksim ran fingers through his hair, sifting and settling the unruly mass. "Papan will have visitors for days wanting to know what the ruckus was."

"Something to talk about." Cherith grinned, fluffing her hair. "I believe it's called a nine-day wonder."

He swallowed. "You're taking the explosion calmly."

Cherith straightened her dress. "I knew you'd save us." Her eyes met his, staggering him with the trust and acceptance in their depths. Gulping, DeMaksim closed his eyes, re-opening them to find her on tiptoe, mouth puckered as she aimed a kiss for his cheek. He twisted, ensuring her lips landed firmly on his, savouring the delicious contact until she dropped back to even footing, staring up at him with soft, doe-like eyes. When her fingers rose to caress her mouth, he reached for her, unable to resist the lure of more, but she swallowed, glanced over his shoulder and shook her head. "Company coming."

Turning, he beheld his father striding towards them. Next to him was Dario, a phalanx of guards close behind.

"DeMaksim!" His father hugged him, then turned to survey Cherith with combined curiosity and fascination. "I'm so very pleased you're here. We were getting worried. We'd heard nothing since you left Castle Synternesse."

"You made it!" Dario smiled, extending his arm for a clasped forearm greeting. "I'm glad you're home today, because Zhu said if you weren't, she was off searching tomorrow."

"There was no way to send messages." DeMaksim drew Cherith

nearer. "This is Lady Cherith Beriaden – we've shared adventures which are still ongoing. Cherith, my father Duke Yanvian Aphiski of Papillion and Duke Dario Eribifax of Garadenya."

"A pleasure, Lady Cherith." Duke Yanvian bowed over her hand.

"Likewise." Dario grinned as he welcomed her.

Cherith blushed. "Thank you both."

Duke Papillion's eyes narrowed. "Was that boundary explosion connected to you? Or should we look further afield?"

"Something chasing you?" Dario's expression was wicked. "I'll save you."

"Perhaps I need saving from myself." DeMaksim's laugh was hollow. "No, I caused the explosion." Dario's brows winged up.

"You?" His father frowned. "But the wards are set to recognise family."

DeMaksim shook his head. "Unless family doesn't look like they're expected to."

"Hmm." Duke Papillion rubbed his chin. "I think we'd better go inside for this story. Besides, your mother and your siblings want to see you."

"Good idea. It's a lengthy tale; easier if I only have to tell it once, especially given time is of the essence. And I'd like to introduce Cherith."

DeMaksim was effusively welcomed by the gathered crowd as they entered the Duchy's gates. Eyes wide, he waved, gripping Cherith's hand supportively as they moved towards the house. Stepping into the foyer, DeMaksim laughed as a new, smaller crowd – comprised of all his sisters and his brother – encircled him and Cherith, all talking at once.

A small bell rang, crystal clear tones transcending the din. At once, the hubbub ceased; the siblings fell back to make a path for their mother. Duchesse Azura's broad smile revealed even white teeth and dimpled cheeks. "DeMaksim! I'm so pleased you're home safely." She drew him in for a hug, pulled his head down and kissed his cheek. Hugging her in return, he noticed when she turned her head to smile at Cherith. "Hello, my dear. Welcome to our home." DeMaksim eased up on the hug, but kept his mother in the circle of his left arm.

"Maman, everyone, this is Lady Cherith Beriaden." His lips turned up warmly as he gazed at his companion. "Cherith, meet my mother: Duchesse Azura, my sisters: Duchesse Zhulija, then Lyssica, Janeska, Tindresse, Armelle and my brother Treymeron."

"Lovely to meet you all." Cherith's smile faltered as everyone spoke at once, creating a cacophony of sound in which nobody could be heard, let alone understood.

To DeMaksim's relief, his mother chimed her crystal bell again. "That's enough. We'll adjourn to the large parlour where everyone will please remember their manners and take turns speaking. Poor Lady Cherith is probably ready to flee." As the foyer emptied, DeMaksim caught sight of Dario, arms crossed.

The Unseelie Beast smirked. "Lots of emotion – last chance to escape."

"Only if Cherith wants to."

"What? Joined at the hip already?"

Cherith raised her hand, drawing DeMaksim's along with it. "No Duke Beastly, just at the wrist." She started down the hall with DeMaksim, who chuckled at Dario's astonished expression. "This I've got to hear!" Dario's hasty footsteps echoed behind them as DeMaksim guided Cherith to the large sitting room.

Once everybody had seated themselves, DeMaksim related his adventures, encouraging Cherith to join in and tell her side of the story. They omitted some private parts but his family listened wide-eyed, fully attentive to every word. When he finished, everyone stared at him in amazement.

Duchesse Azura spoke first. "You can turn into a Dracon? The family rumour is true then!"

"Forget that," Lyssica blurted. "You're mated?"

He nodded. "By the Nageen."

"At least you killed her." Dario nodded. "Good job. She was off her rocker."

"I don't think that's the truly important bit," Zhulija said. "What about Lady Cherith's parents?"

Duke Yanvian cleared his throat. "Zhulija is right. Even if you didn't need Lady Cherith's father to make a potion to break the Nageen's spell, I would wish to come and help rescue her parents. This business with River King Eskavon cannot be allowed to continue. We sacrificed too many lives in the Fae Wars to have the still fragile peace destroyed."

"Absolutely right." Dario frowned. "If he's not a major player among the malcontents, I'd be very surprised. How long did it take you and Lady Cherith to get here, DeMaksim?"

"Four hours, give or take."

Dario's eyebrows rose. "That's good going. Without draconic wings, your father and I won't be as fast on the return."

"That's why I'll carry you both on my back."

Duke Yanvian looked doubtful. "It won't be too much for you?"

DeMaksim chuckled. "No. You'll understand when I change forms."

Duchesse Azura clapped her hands. "Good. I know you'll want to talk and plan, but there's no reason why we still can't continue with tonight's All Hallows bonfire ritual – especially now everyone is home." She looked hopefully at his father. "It's important."

Yanvian smiled softly at her. "Of course my dear. In times of trouble, our traditions are what give us comfort and strength."

His mother clapped her hands together and stood. "Wonderful. You can spend the afternoon planning and then still have time to prepare for tonight."

They spent the afternoon going over the plans with his father and Dario, finessing everyone's role and utilising Dario's expertise in war-strategising. DeMaksim kept squeezing Cherith's hand every time it found its way into his, her worry a rasping in his heart. He understood. He was worried too and they weren't his parents.

They had a subdued dinner with the family and then everyone helped complete the decorations for the All Hallows' Eve celebration before heading out to the specially crafted area where the bonfire was held and where they would share their ancestor stories.

DeMaksim found himself seated, with Cherith and the rest of his family, facing a specially created bonfire in one of the gardens. Hung from poles around the bonfire were hand-carved lanterns containing beeswax candles. He was home for All Hallows' Eve – something he hadn't expected but found himself pleased about. Especially now he had Cherith with him. Each member of the family took turns discussing the ancestor they'd chosen to study from their extensive family tree. The ancestor's name was aired, their life expanded upon, then toasted with a sip of whisky-nectar. When DeMaksim rose to speak, he couldn't help smiling.

"On this All Hallows' Eve, more than any other, I give thanks for my family members, Venstilarquon the Black and his mate Cynamelle Neptulidae, for creating offspring. From their union came our own lives. Long live all family and may our lanterns light their way home!" He raised his glass of whisky-nectar in salute, waited as each member of his family did the same, took a sip, then tossed the rest of the drink on the bonfire. His actions were echoed by everyone, in the ritual they'd created to honour their family members, past and present.

"May our lanterns light their way home!"

CHAPTER SEVENTEEN

CHERITH

*C*herith enjoyed sharing the bonfire ritual with Mak's
family; they were friendly and welcoming. The title of
'Lady,' with which they'd all addressed her had been dispensed
with as quickly as she could say: 'call me Cherith or Cherry.' Eventually the fun wound down and the others began to wander back
to their rooms hoping to get some sleep before it was time to
depart.

"Cherith, it's bedtime."

Mak's soft voice had her straightening and nodding. "Good
idea." Not that she thought she could sleep, even though she was
exhausted. Too much had happened, and her mind was too full of
everything that could go wrong. Mak clasped her free hand in his,
long enough to pull her to her feet and turn them towards the
house. As they walked, Duchesse Azura joined them, tucking her
arm through Cherith's, snugly supportive.

"Thank you for a lovely evening, Ma'am."

"You're very welcome, Cherith." The Duchesse smiled. "I'd like
to offer you the choice of sleeping in the guest room."

Mak sighed. "Maman, I've already explained about the binding.
Did you forget?"

"No dear, I just thought Cherith might prefer something prettier than your male kitted out room. You'd have to endure the change, for the sake of Cherith's comfort."

"Oh, never thought of that. Where would you like to sleep?" he asked Cherith.

She shook her head. "I've no wish to be any trouble, just somewhere neat and clean."

"My room's not clean, Maman?"

Duchesse Azura stiffened. "DeMaksim Yanvian Aphiski! Of course your room's clean and fresh! What sort of housekeepers do you think we have here?"

"Sorry, Maman. I meant no insult ..." When Cherith squeezed Mak's fingers, he trailed off.

"I appreciate the kind thought, Ma'am, but I don't mind staying in Mak's room."

"Are you certain, dear?"

"Yes, thank you." Cherith stifled a laugh at Mak's huffed out breath. "I'm sure I'll be very comfortable."

Duchesse Azura stopped at the foot of a set of stairs. "Very well, I'll say goodnight. Sleep well." She hugged Cherith, then Mak. "I'm thrilled to see you safe, son; and your lady is lovely."

Mak returned the hug, kissing his mother's cheek. "Thanks, Maman. See you in the morning."

Echoing Mak's words, Cherith climbed the circular stairs by his side. The carpeted marble stairwell led to a suite of three rooms in one of the turrets built into the large, rambling, multi storey home. They entered a sitting room, which opened into a bedroom. Off that was a bathing room. The suite was decorated in shades of cream, old gold, rust and jade green; it was welcoming and restful. She bee-lined for the bed, crawled in and made room for Mak as he slid in beside her. "I'm so glad we can magically clean our clothing, otherwise they'd be filthy and reeking by now."

Mak sighed. "They're clean, but I'm mighty sick of them. I've thought about cutting my jacket and shirt off, but I couldn't get anything on over our wrists to replace them. Damn Nageen and her binding."

Cherith nodded, looking away. "Not long before we'll be free of her."

"Yes." Mak stroked her hair. "Try to rest." He continued his soothing motion, but Cherith was too wrought up to relax properly and it was revealed by the tension in her body. He sighed again. "It's not working, is it?"

Wincing, she cracked an eye open. Her face cuddled into Mak's neck; their linked arms were underneath, along with at least half of Mak's body. She mentally face-palmed; she'd ended up sleeping on top of Mak every sleep period since the Nageen had bound them. He must be heartily sick of being squashed. She started to ease away. Mak's hand, the one beneath her, squeezed her leg. Cherith propped herself onto her elbow and peered down. Mak's gorgeous vazel eyes gleamed back at her.

"I know, I'm crushing you again. Sorry."

Mak grinned. "Actually, it's delightful. You're soft in all the right places."

Blushing, Cherith made to pull away, but Mak's other hand cupped her cheek.

"Don't go, please."

She swallowed. "Mak, I know the Nageen messed our lives up but I – I …" She firmed her mouth, gulped, knew this was the moment to tell Mak she wouldn't – couldn't force him to stay with her. "After we save my parents, Papan will make our potion, the link will be nullified and you'll be free again."

He shook his head, one finger stroking the side of her face. "I don't wish to be free of you, Cherith."

She bit her lip. "I – we – you – I understand you think we're mates because, well because Old Venny said so. But really, it's likely just something caused by the Nageen's mating strings."

"I don't agree – is that really what you think?" He shook his head. "After pondering Old Venny's words and carefully considering all of the changes we've gone through, I know we're mates.

The signs are unmistakable but you're in denial for some reason."
He tilted his head. "If you don't want to be mated to me, I'd be
horribly disappointed, because you're amazing, adorable and
wonderful. I've fallen in love with everything about you."

"What?"

"I love you, Cherith."

She stared, lips trembling. "You … you love me?" Her voice
cracked.

"With all that I am." He watched her, a slight smile curling his
lips, eyes aglow with tenderness.

"Oh, Mak." Happiness washed over her. "I do want to be your
mate! I love you too. I just didn't want you feeling trapped and I
thought, I thought it was too good to be true. So strange that we're
accidentally tied together and we turn out to be true mates."

He laughed, his eyes searching hers. "We're meant to be. You,
my gorgeous Undine-Eldwytch, are forever stuck with this Seelie
Fae-male Dracon."

"Best deal ever."

They reached for each other at the same moment, their lips
meeting with time-stopping intensity. Cherith wound her free arm
around Mak's neck, finding his kisses hot, tender; his taste addic-
tive; his scent mesmerising. His free arm encircled her waist, hand
moving down to her hip and back to her waist before sliding up
her rib cage. Their linked hands were in a constant battle as they
fought to touch each other.

Cherith swept her tongue out, licking Mak's lower lip. Mouth
opening, his tongue flicked to meet hers in a tangling, taste-teasing
duel. She thrilled to the feel of his sex lengthening and hardening
against her leg and hip. His free hand left her ribs to pull the
shoulder of her dress aside and down, exposing one breast.
Cupping it, his fingers rubbed a circle around the tip, then flicked
the nipple. Cherith flung her head back, gasping as delightful
sensations zinged through her. His head dropped, teeth grazing
the tingling peak before his warm, wet mouth nibbled and kissed
and licked its way from one breast, nuzzling under fabric to find

and tend to her other breast, his hand plumping and stroking and shaping as he went.

The sweet, plundering kisses left her senses spinning and her breasts delightfully sensitive. Desire was a burning ember, coiling low in her belly and sparking up her spine. Cherith wriggled until she straddled Mak fully, then tilted her hips to rub herself against the fullness of his groin. His choked exclamation was music to her ears as she fisted her free hand in his leather jacket and slid against his heavily swollen sex again and again. When his wet inferno of a mouth resumed adoring her breasts, his hand slipped between her legs and pushed aside her underwear, his fingers tickling through her damp curls. He circled the sensitive nub gently but firmly, rubbing and stroking the slick bud, building the intensity, twisting his fingers to find her sweet centre, repeating the actions over and over until she splintered into a million shards of shining glory. Cherith mewed when the fiery pleasure shot through her, whimpered, shivered and shook, before finally sagging in Mak's arms, limp and overcome.

With a throaty sound of approval, Mak raised his head, dragged Cherith close and kissed her again. A series of fierce, open-mouthed kisses across her flesh; tasting and teasing, his lips nibbling and savouring, licking and sucking. Senses sparkling with love and pleasure, she met him kiss for kiss, releasing her grasp on his jacket to slide her hand down to his groin and pluck at his trousers.

"Off." As the intense longing and the electric aching renewed, Cherith's voice was a frantic mumble between the searing tangling of their lips and tongues. "I want to touch you, Mak! I need all of you." She stroked his length; his hips bucked and frustrated annoyance flooded her. "Clothes off!" The command accompanied a burst of her fiery will and to the astonishment of both of them, they were instantly nude.

The passion in Mak's eyes intensified as he savoured her nakedness, his roving gaze almost as physical as his available hand. "You're so gorgeous, my darling, so adorably, unbelievably gorgeous." His fingers returned to her centre, their movement re-igniting sensations of pleasurable intensity. Cherith lunged towards him, kissing and nipping his jaw, his chin, his neck; inhaling the delicious scent that she would always identify as Mak's. Her hand between them, gripped his erection, stroking the rigidity, caressing the soft tip. He moaned, thrusting upwards in her clasp. Propelling her hips forward, Cherith surged along the heated length of him, then back, raising herself so that she could guide him into her desperate, aching core. Mak grasped her hips, helping her seat herself.

They gasped in unison as she flexed around his shaft, sliding down, accepting him into her body, lowering herself until she was fully seated and they were groin to groin. She swallowed, eyes closed, feeling wonderfully, deliciously full.

"Oh, blue bla-azes ..." His words trailed off in a gasp.

Cherith's eyelids drifted open again and she stared into the face of her mate. Words taught to her by her Eldwytch sire surged from her memory into her mouth, spilling from her lips. "You, DeMaksim Yanvian Aphiski, are my mate. I see you. I accept you. I take you as mine and give myself unto you. There is no other, there will be no other. I willingly twine my soul to yours and seal our lives together." Her throat rippled. "Will you say those words back to me, Mak?"

"It would be my honour, darling." With a little prompting, he spoke the vows. As he concluded, the tension snapped taut between them, the pleasure in their bodies spiking until they could do nothing but succumb. He drove up, she pushed down, they pulled back, flexing and repeating the mind-numbing, senses steal-ing, delight of loving each other until Cherith convulsed, again and again, in helpless rapture. As the waves of bliss overtook her, Mak stiffened beneath her. Her pleasure achieved new heights as he climaxed, pulsing hot and hard inside her, his fingers digging into her hip bones like claws.

Following her instincts, Cherith bared her small fangs and dove on Mak, biting into his pectoral muscles until she drew blood. His claw rose from her hip with traces of her blood decorating the tip. Eyes locked on each other, both smiling, she swept her tongue across her fangs while he sucked his claw.

Lightning struck. A sizzling whiplash shot between them, illuminating their bodies in glorious splendour, creating a glowing mate-cord from one to the other.

"What?" Mak's voice emerged as a croak.

Cherith managed to gasp the words, "Eldwytch mating magic."

"Another thing to be thankful for this All Hallows' Eve."

She nodded. He was right. There would never be another All Hallows' Eve like this one. And even though she was still worried about her parents, in this moment, lying quiescent and content in Mak's arms, she allowed herself not only to feel this moment of happiness, but to revel in it.

Kissing her brow, he held her close, murmuring words of love in her ear until they both dozed.

CHAPTER EIGHTEEN

DEMAKSIM

They made love again after dozing for an hour, put the wall to good use on their way to the shower and enjoyed a very long, involved shower before towelling each other off. Their drying took even longer than their washing routine, but they finally reached the point of needing clothes.

DeMaksim traced a finger along Cherith's collarbone and down to one breast. "You magicked our old clothes away somewhere – even if we had them, how do we get them on, over and around this infernal linking string?"

"I don't even know how I disposed of them." Cherith sucked her bottom lip between her teeth and rolled it, releasing it with a smacking sound. "But I magicked them off, so it stands to reason I'd be able to magic them back." Cherith frowned. "Clothes return to us." Nothing happened. She tried a second time, and a third, becoming first concerned. "There has to be a way." Then annoyed. "Why the swamp-slush isn't it working?"

"We'll have to try non-magical dressing." DeMaksim pursed his lips, eyeing Cherith's breasts. "Although our chests will be naked – not so bad for me, but I'd rather keep your loveliness private.

Perhaps we can rip a shirt open and pin it back together somehow? Or wind bandages around you ..."

"No!" Cherith bared her fangs in a snarl. "No, no, no! I want us properly dressed. I want clothes on both of us and I want that now!" Both suddenly fully clothed, boots and all, they stood gaping at each other.

DeMaksim looked down. "You did it!" He grinned, then kissed her.

They headed downstairs to meet the others and grab something quick to eat.

Once they were done, everyone crowded out through the door to see him change.

Treymeron shrugged as they walked outside together. "He always showed patches of brown scales, so he's probably brown all over."

Duchesse Azura shook her head. "You haven't been listening Trey; lots of things have changed for DeMaksim since he was last here; one of the most wonderful is how he's brought Cherith into the family."

DeMaksim exchanged a glance with Cherith, who was blushing. "I'll lift you up when I change." She nodded; they both grinned and DeMaksim sought his alter ego, becoming enveloped in a swirl of sparkling fog before coalescing into his opalescent blue-green draconic form. Mouths gaped as he towered over the lot of them, his hide a mix of scales and feathery fronds with Cherith perched on his foreleg.

"Not a brown scale on him from this angle. Your memory's gone." Dario chuckled as he ribbed Trey.

Duke Yanvian massaged his jaw. "Parts of you look like you're draped in weeds, yet it's feathery and scaly too. Amazing!"

Armelle came closer to pat his hide, low on one powerful hind leg. "I think you're some sort of water Dracon."

"Because Cherith is part Undine." Janeska's eyes were wide.

Tindresse had circled completely around them. "But also Eldwytch. So fascinating."

"I agree." Lyssica walked to where Cherith sat. "I'm so glad for you both. Welcome sister."

"Wonderful to see DeMaksim in this form, but it's time to go," Duchesse Azura said, gesturing at the moon which had travelled across the sky, telling them her words were true. DeMaksim helped Cherith make herself comfortable, then crouched to allow his father and Dario to climb up after they'd said farewell to their mates and family. With a bit of manoeuvring, they finally settled on the back of his neck. It felt strange having riders, but their weight wasn't an issue. Bunching his haunches, he leaped skywards, wings drumming strongly for altitude, before he levelled off and struck out for the Dark Reaches.

The journey to the Whortlebog seemed to take forever. The tension rising from everyone permeated the air like a black cloud. Wings beating strongly, DeMaksim scanned the shadowed land below. With draconic night vision he had no trouble identifying the landmarks, and when the Mirkdowd River finally appeared beneath them, his internal clock indicated they were well within their time line. *"Cherith, we're near the Whortlebog: do you know where the Dracon stone is Venny spoke of?"*

She pointed. *"To the east, not far from where Whortle Creek spills out into the bog."* Banking right, DeMaksim flew on. When he saw the signs of a swamp in the distance, he began looking for the Dracon-shaped rock. He dropped closer to the forest, seeking to make himself harder to detect, in case there were enemies this close to the rendezvous even though they were a few hours early.

Spying the rock, he circled once, marvelling at how realistically draconic it appeared, before back-winging down to land in the adjacent clearing. An ancient forest towered around them; massive oaks, elms and ash reached for the sky, some of the green leaves interspersed with reds and oranges as autumn moved in.

As planned, nobody moved while they reconnoitred their surroundings; each of them focusing eyes and senses in different directions and calling soft-voiced acknowledgments after completing their check: "Clear."

Dario spoke from his position on DeMaksim's neck. "I'll dismount first, Yanvian will stand guard, then I'll be on alert while he descends." They'd agreed Dario would take charge since, of the two experienced warriors, he was a current Queen's agent while Duke Yanvian was retired. Crouching low, DeMaksim waited as Dario scooted sideways, then slid to the ground; Duke Yanvian followed soon after.

Lowering Cherith to her feet, DeMaksim swirled back to his Fae-form. "Okay?" She nodded.

Dario gestured. "Okay, into the trees." His low-voiced orders continued. "Mak, Cherith, you're watching from here, look for movement, or anything out of place. Yanvian, scout a shallow left circle around the clearing. I'll do a deeper right circle." Duke Yanvian nodded and within seconds the two Fae-males had faded into the bushes.

Not long after, an unusual flapping breeze in the treetops caused DeMaksim to glance up. A familiar black Dracon appeared from the north-west, flying low. It circled as he'd done, then cruised in to land next to the rock before crouching to unload passengers. First down was a tall Fae-male with tawny hair who quickly unsheathed a sword and, balancing on the balls of his feet, spun slowly.

Venstilarquon the Black snorted a smoke trail. "Stand down, Athys. I don't want you skewering any of my family."

The swordsman retained his vigilance. "We can't be too careful, Ancient One."

"Yeah, but the only people I scent are those we came to meet." Old Venny narrowed his eyes, staring straight at Cherith and DeMaksim, despite them being concealed by trees. "Come out, you two. I won't let Athys stab you." He swung his head to the swordsman. "Put your pig-sticker away!"

As DeMaksim and Cherith stepped from their concealment, the regal female still astride Venny spoke. "Oh, do as he says, Athys. I'm certain his sense of smell is superior to ours."

Athys sighed. "Majesty, I can't protect you if I'm not allowed to do my job." Deep brown eyes settled on Cherith and DeMaksim, flickering over them, assessing, the sword weaving a tight pattern.

Old Venny muttered something unintelligible; Athys responded with a sharp look, but he huffed, lowering his sword. Old Venny nodded. "Mak, Cherith, good to see you. Where—"

"Here." His father stepped from the trees to flank Cherith and DeMaksim.

"Good. What about—"

"I'm here also." Dario came from behind Old Venny.

Spinning with a curse, sword rising, Athys halted as he saw Dario. Sheathing the blade, he stepped to meet the warrior's proffered forearm greeting. "Trust you to sneak up behind me, Beast." He raised his voice. "Micron, weren't you on rear watch?"

Dario smiled mirthlessly. "I made myself known to Her Majesty and Micron."

"That he did." Another male voice, rife with amusement, called from high on Old Venny.

Athys rolled his eyes. "I need to be able to rely on you, Micron."

There came a loud female sigh. "Dario, do help me down. These two could be at it for hours."

Dario bowed. "At once, Your Majesty."

"Both unfair and untrue, Your Majesty." Athys moved to join Dario in helping the queen descend from Old Venny's back. Her hair was a continuous, playful pattern of colour and light as it morphed from golden blonde to pale blue, then all shades of blue to midnight and back again. Bright blue eyes brimming with power and charisma flashed over them all.

"My Queen." Cherith dropped into a curtsy, her linked wrist stretching to where DeMaksim bowed, alongside his father.

"Rise." Unseelie Queen Maerovana rubbed her hands briskly. "Thank you and well-met." She cast amused eyes over Duke Yanvian. "I'll have such fun informing Cousin Dia how one of her subjects is mated to one of mine – again – and her subjects both children of yours, Sir Duke."

"I'm glad that you are enjoying the dichotomy, Your Majesty."

Duke Yanvian bowed again. "I'm simply a father pleased to have two children achieve true matings, regardless of the origins of their partners. I didn't shed blood for Fae unity, only to turn my back on its fulfillment."

"Well spoken, Duke Papillion." Queen Maerovana twitched the skirts of her long green gown and turned up the collar of her cloak. "Let's move closer to the meeting point." She glanced at Old Venny who had resumed his Fae-shape and was inspecting the draconically shaped stone outcrop. "Your mate, Lady Cynamelle will be there, with the remaining two offspring of the captives, you said, Venny?"

Old Venny patted the rock, then turned away. "Cyn tells me they've already arrived, but haven't yet found any traces of Eskavon." He gestured east. "That way." Arranging themselves with Dario and Yanvian on point, Cherith and DeMaksim followed Athys, Queen Maerovana, and Micron, with Old Venny bringing up the rear. Moving into the trees, DeMaksim paused, looking back at the large rock dominating the clearing.

"Very detailed rock, Gramps. Is it a carving or a natural phenomenon?"

Old Venny glanced at him, mouth turned down at the corners. "That's Kadendall. One of my sons; he offended the wrong entity. I suppose you could call him a natural phenomenon."

CHAPTER NINETEEN

CHERITH

*C*herith was relieved to arrive where Becks and Cassie waited with Cyn. The trio were seated with backs to tree trunks, an array of large shrubs and bushes separating and obscuring their view of the Whortlebog. Cassie leapt to her feet, bolted for Cherith and hugged her fiercely. "Thank the River Goddess you made it safely Cherry! Hi Mak."

Becks followed. "We—" His eyes widened as he identified Unseelie Queen Maerovana. "Your Majesty!" He immediately bowed. Mouth open, Cassie released Cherith and executed a curtsy.

"I beg pardon, Your Majesty." Her throat rippled as she swallowed.

Queen Maerovana gestured. "Please rise. I gather you're Cascade and Beckett Beriaden?"

Becks smiled. "Yes, Your Majesty. Thank you for assisting us."

The Queen's smile was wintry. "I'm not happy with Eskavon's potentially treasonous behaviour, not to mention him kidnapping loyal subjects. He and I will be having *words*."

Old Venny, his arm around Cyn, barked a laugh. "More than words, I'm thinking."

Queen Maerovana glanced his way. "Very perceptive, Ancient One. Greetings Lady Cynamelle, a pleasure to have your company."

Cyn smiled, curtsying. "Lovely to see you, Your Majesty."

"I wish it was under better circumstances." The queen's fists landed on her hips. "Old Venny told me the basics of the plan, but I imagine you've fine tuned it, Dario?"

"You know your subject too well, Your Majesty."

She waved her hand. "Tell me what you've come up with."

Dario swept his hair behind one pointed ear. "Certainly, Your Majesty. We tried to think of as many scenarios as possible. The Whortlebog has only one area of firm ground, a tongue of land extending into the bog. The plan we go with will depend largely on which direction Eskavon comes from and whether he brings the elder Beriadens with him."

The Queen frowned. "Why wouldn't he have his victims with him?"

"No idea." Dario shrugged. "But it's a possibility we can't ignore. As for direction, he may approach from safe ground or from the bog. Lady Delta is water based but Lord Istondir is not, so if Eskavon brings them through the bog, it'll have to be by boat. There's also the issue of how many he'll have in his retinue and whether those Fae are also traitors, or merely led astray by their River King, thinking they're doing the right thing."

Cassie sounded bewildered. "Why would anyone think kidnapping was the right thing?"

"A very good question." The Queen tapped her foot. "Continue, Lord Dario."

"Right." Dario rubbed his jaw. "As far as we know, Eskavon wants DeMaksim because he's decided Mak is a spy for the joint Queendom – that tells us at least two things. Number one: Eskavon has something to hide; number two: he's not a fan of said joint Queendom. He also wants Cherith because he believes she ran off with the supposed spy, instead of watching him as per orders – even though DeMaksim tells me he was made aware of the Nageen roping Cherith and Mak together."

Cyn shook her head. "Eskavon must be insane. It's inconceivable that Cassie and Becks would be willing to swap their sister for their parents, nor would Delta and Istondir want to be freed from captivity in exchange for any of their children."

"Exactly." Dario grinned at her. "Even if he's annoyed at Cherith's alleged behaviour, he may simply want to chastise her. Unfortunately, thanks to the Nageen, if Eskavon insists on taking Mak, he'll get Cherith too."

The queen levelled Dario with a frosty stare. "Eskavon gets no-one."

Grimacing, Dario returned her gaze. "That's the core of the plan, Your Majesty, but there are no guarantees."

The queen's glare intensified. "That was an order, Beast. Make it so."

Dario nodded crisply. "Our best strategy is to take him by surprise and keep him off balance. If we station people in the trees nearest the land-spit, as well as the bog, we should be able to prevent him escaping. He'll be expecting a party of four people: Becks and Cassie with Mak and Cherith. If you're agreeable, my Queen, I suggest that you wear your hooded cloak, pretend to be Cassie and reveal your true self when you consider it appropriate."

Queen Maerovana's smile made Cherith shiver. When the queen spoke, her voice was just as deadly. "Yes, Dario, I like that part of the plan, but one person wearing a hooded cloak will be a bit odd, won't it?"

"Yes, that's why we brought four cloaks, enough for the whole focal party." Dario smirked. "And, that will hopefully be where he loses control of the situation – he won't be expecting Your Majesty's presence. It'll also be when we discover how deep the rot goes. The rest of us will be positioned with regard to our strengths."

"I already have a cloak."

"With all due respect, Your Majesty." Cherith smiled. "Your

cloak is of velvet, while the cloaks we brought are every day wear. It would be better if you matched the rest of the party."

"Smart." The queen nodded approvingly at Cherith. "Of course, I will."

Dario turned to Cassie. "Are you willing to be our bog liaison? Not in the mud, but in one of the fresh water flows that bisect it – with Queen Maerovana masquerading as yourself, you'll be the only water-based person not in the focal party and we need all directions guarded."

"Yes, of course." Cassie's eyes were huge. "But what do I do?"

Dario's lips twisted. "Hopefully nothing, but if things fall apart and you find yourself in the thick of the action, you'll have to act as you see fit. With luck, Becks will be able to assist you." He glanced around. "Everybody will need to react to however the confrontation pans out. Eskavon may surrender, or he may seek to escape. Micron, Athys and I will form a loose circle to prevent Eskavon leaving along the land-spit." Dario glanced at Old Venny and Cyn. "I doubt if there'll be sky action, but if there is—"

"Don't fret, we'll be there backing up whoever needs help." Old Venny gestured. "Cyn's a fantastic archer and she brought along her bow and a loaded quiver.

Dario rubbed his hands. "Another unexpected bonus!"

"I'm nervous." Cassie clutched Cherith's arm.

"We all are, but you'll do great." Cherith smiled at her sister.

Mak gave Cassie an encouraging pat on the shoulder. "Your Maman and Papan will be so proud." Cassie's grip eased, she nodded, smiling weakly.

"Time to go." Dario appeared before them. "Cassie, you ready?"

Cassie saluted. "On it!" With a last squeeze of Cherith's arm, she set off.

Frowning, Cherith watched Cassie disappear into the undergrowth to make her stealthy way to the bog; she hoped her sister stayed safe. Sighing, she allowed Duke Yanvian to help her don a cloak, while Dario assisted Mak. By the time she and Mak were ready, Queen Maerovana and Becks were cloaked, hooded and waiting.

Dario looked from person to person. "Everyone's ready? Fine, let's do this."

"Wait!" Cherith grasped Dario's arm. "Shouldn't Mak look like a prisoner? Eskavon won't believe he's here willingly."

"Hmm, good point." Dario scratched his head, glancing around.

"I might have something," Duke Yanvian said, digging into his backpack. "Here." He straightened, holding a length of rope. "Never know when a good bit of rope will come in handy."

Dario's brow cleared. "Excellent!" He formed a loop and pushed it onto Mak's linked hand. "Just hold it, nobody will know the difference until it's too late." He linked the rope to Mak's other hand and formed a second loop. Once Mak had hold of it, he trailed the rope end across to Becks and handed it over. "You're the obvious choice for jailer. You and the queen follow Cherith and Mak as if you're herding them. Good luck, everyone."

Conscious of their escorts, Cherith and Mak walked slowly clear of the concealing forest undergrowth. Before them lay the open ground which continued until it became a tiny peninsula pushing into the Whortlebog. The sky was paling as dawn approached.

The smell of the sulphurous and methane gasses produced by decaying plant matter hit them hard. "Oh, River Goddess!" Cherith switched to breathing through her mouth. "I'd forgotten how intensely it stinks."

"Play your parts." The queen murmured. "There may be watchers." They continued walking in silence until they reached the end of the spit, where they clustered, looking down at the swamp. Beneath them, at the base of the rock was a layer of crusty grey mud; a little further out was clear flowing water, then more mud, followed by tussocks of grass and reeds at the feet of some scrubby, windswept bushes. Beyond, the pattern of mud, water channels, tussocks, reeds and scrub continued across the bog like a convoluted maze, with no people in sight.

"Okay, it's showtime." Becks tugged gently on the rope, voice quiet. "Mak, follow my lead, I'll push you down; pretend you don't want to go, then give in and sit, acting like a reluctant prisoner. Cherry you drop and sit next to him, while Her – ah, um, false-Cassie and I stand sentinel over you."

Holding back a grin as the tiny struggle played out, Cherith lowered herself to sit cross-legged on the ground. She watched Mak glaring up at Becks and 'Cassie'. The latter had her arms crossed. Becks' gaze darted over Cherith's head towards the forest, then lowered to her. He shook his head. "Stop smiling Cherry."

"I'm trying."

He prodded her with the toe of his boot and started shouting. "And as for you Cherry, you've been really stupid!" Cherith was startled; Becks waved his fist in front of her face.

She reared back. "W-what? Why?" Was that squeak her voice?

"Instead of being a loyal Dark Reaches Unseelie Undine, doing the job laid out for you by your River King, you sided with this spy!" He frowned heavily. "What possessed you? Were you bewitched? If so, Papan could break an enchantment by crafting a potion, but your rank idiocy has caused both Maman and Papan to be arrested. I hope you're pleased with yourself. It's no wonder the River King is incensed."

"I couldn't have said it better myself." Their attention jerked up as River King Eskavon strolled across the spit of land towards them. Behind him marched Aquinal, leading a mixed group of Nixies, Water Sprites, Undines, Kelpies and other Water Fae. Eskavon was clothed in trousers of tightly woven brown bulrushes, a jerkin of green weeds and a cloak that looked like rippling water with foam-bedecked edges. Atop his sandy hair, he wore a crown of a green quartz, studded with small nuggets of gold and gemstones. He shook his head. "Such a disappointment, Cherry, both to me and to your parents." Cherith swallowed. "Nothing to say, sweet Cherry? Tsk, tsk."

Becks cleared his throat. "As you see, Your Majesty, Cassie and

I have brought the spy to you. Where are our parents? You said they'd be released."

Eskavon studied him. "You look very Eldwytch, just as your sisters look very Undine." His mouth turned down. "I never trusted Delta after she mated an Eldwytch Mage. Unnatural." He hissed the word. "And mixed triplets?" He hawked and spat. "Even more unnatural. Mixed breeds, mixed sexes in one birth – that is not the way of *my* Water Fae – how can I be certain of loyalty?" He shook his head again. "Cherry has proved my point so aptly with her behaviour." He switched his gaze to Mak and his mouth twisted. "This creature beside you must be the spy who's given us so much trouble. Do you spy for the Queens, Seelie filth?"

"Spy? What in blue blazes?" Mak glared at the River King. "As I've explained time and again, I came here on a personal matter, but I'd like to know how I can be a spy with Fae unity in place? The queens rule jointly over a combined Queendom, so what're you talking about?"

"Fae unity!" Eskavon snarled. "We don't honour that sort of pond scum here! None of my people do if they know what's good for them."

"Is that so, Eskavon?" Queen Maerovana threw back the hood of her cloak, her ever-changing hair glinting in the sunlight. "The vow of fealty you swore, to both myself and my cousin, Queen Dianathke, means nothing to you then?"

He gasped, paling. "Your Majesty!" Behind him, more gasps sounded, followed by lots of murmurs. Most of the Water Fae lowered themselves towards the ground in either a bow or curtsy.

Without taking her eyes from Eskavon, the queen called out to the genuflecting Water Fae. "If you are loyal subjects of the Queendom, you may rise and leave. My knights will confirm your faithfulness and allow you passage once you convince them."

He glared. "They're my people!"

She smirked. "Are they, indeed?" He risked a glance behind him, swearing viciously when he saw the stampede of Water Fae aiming for the forest. A line of fire sprang up, preventing a mass exodus.

Three tall figures stood in the only clear passage between the flames. The hair of one of the figures roiled with red flame.

"The Unseelie Beast!"

"A very patriotic subject, Eskavon, unlike you."

Eskavon's lip curled. "A fanny-licker!"

Queen Maerovana pursed her lips, her stare arctic. "An interesting idea, but I've missed my chance – his true mate would probably get very unpleasant if I tried to follow up on it." Her eyes narrowed. "Now, tell me where Lord and Lady Beriaden are?"

Eskavon grinned nastily. "Out there." He waved at the Whortlebog. "In a boat with a hole in it and they're tied together. If they're not found before the boat sinks, they'll die."

Cherith stiffened as her brother shouted, "That wasn't the deal you made."

"What do I care for deals?" The River King's unpleasant grin broadened.

"How a dishonourable piece of shite like you fooled us enough to command our allegiance, I'll never understand." Cherith bristled. "Anyway, Maman is an Undine, she can't drown."

"No, she won't drown, but she'll starve to death." He paused. "Over a number of days and all while she's bound to the body of her mate – who *can* and *will* drown." He smirked. "So very sad."

Becks went for Eskavon's throat, but Queen Maerovana grasped his arm, even while the River King danced aside. His retreat brought him closer to Cherith; grinning nastily he kicked her lower leg.

Cherith cried out.

"Bastard!" Mak grabbed Cherith's hand, pulling her closer to him.

Becks stared at the Queen. "Why'd Your Majesty stop me?"

"He provoked you on purpose. Leave him to me." She returned her attention to Eskavon, just as he lunged after Cherith.

"You've ruined everything, you little half-breed bitch!" He aimed a knee at her face. "I'll destroy you and kill this Seelie scum you ran away with!"

"Mak is mine." Dodging the knee, Cherith drove her fist between Eskavon's legs.

"Aargh!" The River King bellowed, curling over, hands flying to his groin. His crown toppled from his head to roll across the ground. "My crown!" His voice emerged a tortured croak. One hand cupping his groin, the other reaching for the lost diadem, he staggered a step, then dropped to his knees and fell sideways, writhing in pain.

Stooping, Queen Maerovana caught the bejewelled circlet, looping it over her wrist. "It's no longer your crown, Eskavon. For your crimes, I decree you no longer River King of the Mirkdowd River or its tributaries." She made a violent wrenching gesture in the space between the coronet on her arm and where Eskavon lay. There was a sharp crack which reverberated and echoed from one end of the Queendom to the other. It belled across the sky, roared over the land and ripped through the waters; Queen Maerovana's justice a whirlwind that tore at clothing and sent hair flying as she snapped Eskavon's psychic link to the river kingdom. His drawn-out shriek of agony caused those near him to shudder. The Water Fae still in the clearing fell to the ground, their connection with their King abruptly cut. Cherith staggered, kept upright and conscious by her link to Mak, as everyone else – her siblings included – were felled by the blow.

"You may have been born to this crown," the queen said into the sudden quiet. "But it's still a division of the Fae Demesnes as a greater whole – and the Fae Demesnes are united under the combined crowns of Queens Dianathke and Maerovana. Let all who gainsay us remember this day and beware."

Terror trembling inside her as she took in all the unconscious Water Fae, Cherith turned to Mak. "Maman and Papan – what if the breaking of the crown affected Maman too? They'll drown. We have to find them. Now."

Mak caught her close, his mouth in her hair as he rocked her. "We'll find them, darling. Two of us are Dracons, remember? We'll find them, I promise."

CHAPTER TWENTY

DEMAKSIM

*M*orphing to Dracon, he waited for Cherith to settle herself, then leaped for the sky with a massive downstroke of his wings. *"Watch for Gramps, I need to bring him up to date."*

They scanned the sky, looking for a large winged shape. *"Over there!"* Cherith pointed. Following the angle of her finger, DeMaksim saw the unmistakeable draconic shape. Altering direction, he flew to meet the black Dracon, circling to fly alongside.

"What's happening?" Old Venny tilted his scaled head.

"Cherith's parents are tied up in some sort of sinking boat. Not only that – the queen broke the River King's bond to his people and it felled most of them. We don't know how far the shockwave went. If it felled Cherith's mother, she won't be able to keep them afloat when the boat sinks. They'll die if we don't find them quickly. You go the east and I'll take the west." DeMaksim bellowed.

"Got it." Venstilarquon banked and flew east.

"I'll keep watch my side and you watch the other one." Cherith sounded breathless. The trees and shrubs which survived in the

slimy morass made searching more difficult, forcing them to fly up and down the water channels in the bog, following the twists and turns in the maze of mud and water. The search took them further and further from their starting point, and their efforts startled quite a few ducks and other water fowl, who swam or flew away, quacking or peeping in anxiety as a large creature overflew them.

Hours later, Cherith pointed. *"Could that be them?"* They were searching a side channel, the solid ground of the meeting place nowhere nearby. DeMaksim dropped lower, circling for a better look. Beneath them, a decrepit bark canoe sat low in the water. The bodies of the two people inside faced each other, their upturned faces struggling to stay above the water lapping high on their necks. *"Yes!"* Cherith flung a happy grin over her shoulder.

"They need to see you to understand I'm no danger to them." DeMaksim went in low, with Cherith waving and hallooing madly at her parents.

"How are we going to save them?" Cherith twisted her head to stare anxiously at him.

"Hold tight." Circling again, DeMaksim swooped, snatched the rope binding the trapped couple in the claws of his free paw, then beat his wings strongly, rising with his new burden. Fortunately, their movements were minimal, just enough for DeMaksim to see they were alive. As he circled into a rising thermal, the ungainly canoe beneath, buffeted by the downdraught of his wings, capsized and sank leaving only sluggish ripples to mark the place where it had been.

"Oh, my goddess!" Cherith clasped her throat.

"I've got them." With his extra, very awkward burden, DeMaksim was grateful the way back could be flown in a straight line.

"Look." Cherith pointed again. *"There's your Gramps."* The black dragon coasted to join them; they were surprised to see he cupped a bedraggled and muddy Cassie in one claw.

The tongue of firm land came into view, along with the small rise between the water and the forest. Fae-people sat or lay everywhere, either still or barely moving. Sighting them, a figure DeMaksim identified as Dario, ensured an area near the tip of the tiny peninsula was clear enough for he and Old Venny to land.

"Athys, help needed here!" Dario bellowed towards the forest. The Fae-male stood up and sprinted towards them.

Settling slowly, DeMaksim was relieved when Dario and Athys slid the bundle of Cherith's parents free of his aching foreleg and lowered them to the ground.

"What's all this?" DeMaksim stared around, at what was now a makeshift camp full of moaning Fae, in bewilderment. He reverted to his Fae form, assisting Cherith to gain her balance when she seemed a bit wobbly.

Dario produced a dagger to cut the wet ropes binding the Beri-adens. "Many of the Water Fae have gone into shock since you left." He looked to Cherith. "How are you coping?"

She looked at him doubtfully. "I'm okay. Just a bit unsteady."

Dario frowned. "Could be you're getting energy from your link to DeMaksim." He turned to Venstilarquon who was crouching to allow Cyn to climb down. "Is that Cassie? She's covered in mud."

"Found her mired in the bog, barely noticed her waving." Old Venny, with Cyn's assistance, laid Cassie gently on the ground. "She hasn't moved much, seems dazed."

Cherith gave a tiny laugh. "Poor Cassie; one of the rescue team and she had to be rescued too!" She stared across at her parents, her heart in her eyes. "Maman? Papan?"

Dario met her worried gaze. "They're alive, but weak. Of the two of them, your Papan is in better condition."

DeMaksim felt her fingers grip his tightly. "He wasn't a subject of the River King."

"That helps. Your Maman is in a similar state to the majority of the Water Fae."

Queen Maerovana arrived. "I've started feeding my energy into the Mirkdowd sub-kingdom loop. There have been no fatalities and I want to keep it that way, but we need supplies.

Venny? DeMaksim? Are you willing to fly some in?"

~

Craning her neck, Cherith peered into the large kettle simmering over the open-air pit. "Is the potion done yet, Papan?" DeMaksim closed his free hand around her shoulder, steadying her as she stood on tiptoe. *Careful, darling.* She flashed him a loving smile.

Grinning, Istondir Beriaden tapped his daughter on the tip of her nose with one of his long, elegant fingers. "So impatient. It'll be ready when it's ready and not before."

Watching them, DeMaksim was pleased to see Cherith had the kind of close relationship with her parents that he had with his. It made him realise anew that the differences between Seelie and Unseelie were not unbridgeable.

"I hope you're not overdoing things, Papan." Cherith wagged her finger. "You didn't have to prepare the anti-Nageen potion today."

Istondir hugged his daughter. "I'm fine, and a night's rest has done wonders for my state of mind. I'm also delighted to discover such a wonderful son-in-law. The least I can do is help break the Nageen's curse." He waved his hands around. "We've fed and helped all the suffering Water Fae, so I've the time, the ingredients and the inclination." He eyed her. "Perhaps you should sit down, too. You're pale; I know the broken bond with Eskavon must be affecting you as much as it has Cassie, Becks and your Maman."

Cherith glanced lovingly at her mate. "I'm not as badly off as most. Mak has been pushing energy through our link."

"As I said, an excellent choice. I was helping your Maman in a similar fashion after she came close to losing consciousness in the boat. A partnership as well as a mating – the best kind." Istondir clapped an approving hand on DeMaksim's shoulder, before returning to the cooking pot and peering in. "Ah, the colour is changing. Almost done." He stirred the brew with a wooden paddle, watching it gently bubbling. Presently, he ladled the syrupy concoction into a bowl. "You both need to drink some, then pour it over the strings. But let it cool first; it'll scald you right now." He prodded around their joined wrists, long fingers searching. "Huh, I can't see the binding, but I can feel it."

DeMaksim nodded. "I can see it when I'm in my draconic form – not that seeing it is much help."

After the brew was sufficiently cool, Istondir held the bowl out to Cherith. "Two mouthfuls, then pass it to Mak." She did as directed, pulling a face as she swallowed. Then it was Mak's turn. He tried not to gag over the thick, tasteless brew, then returned the bowl to Istondir. Cherith's father ladled more potion into the dish, then began basting it onto the cords, adding more and more as the potion formed a white lather. The outline of the binding ropes became visible under the froth. "Now we'll wash this off and, with luck, the binding will disintegrate." He looked around, caught sight of his son talking with Dario and Old Venny. "Becks, would you bring a bowl of water, please?"

While Becks fetched water, Old Venny and Dario moved closer.

"Here you are, Papan." Becks carried a wide-mouthed jug. "Fresh out of the river."

Istondir nodded. "Thank you. Please hold it under the lathered area." Becks complied and Istondir firmly pushed Cherith and DeMaksim's lathered wrists into the container. The brew foamed violently.

Old Venny rubbed his hands. "Here we go!"

Cherith gasped as the lather seeped away into the surrounding water. "It's working!" But when, at Istondir's urging, they lifted their wrists from the water, the link was intact – the only difference …

"The binding's red!"

Cherith's pale face flushed. "But, it's still there! Why didn't it work? What'll we do now?"

"Shh, shh, Cherry," Istondir soothed. "The cords are now visible. We'll lather them again and they'll surely disintegrate."

But they didn't and Cherith burst into heart-rending sobs, tears flowing down her face. Her father and DeMaksim both moved to hug her and when neither backed down, the embrace ended up being three-way.

DeMaksim met Istondir's gaze over the top of Cherith's head; Istondir looked as miserable as he felt. Despite their best efforts, the cursed binding of the dead Nageen still existed. *Are we destined to spend the rest of our immortal lives chained together?* Sighing, DeMaksim dropped a kiss on Cherith's hair. Her tears dripped onto his hand. Water hadn't worked, maybe his flame? He knew he couldn't harm himself with his flame, but what about Cherith? Old Venny would likely know.

"Hey Gramps? Will my flame harm Cherith?"

Old Venny shook his head. "As I said when you went through my portal, neither you nor your mate can harm each other with your powers – you thinking of flaming the strings?"

"Yes." DeMaksim's brow furrowed. "I haven't tried it because I worried I'd hurt Cherith. Let's try. Istondir, could you move back, please?"

When Istondir joined Becks, Dario and Old Venny, DeMaksim directed a fine stream of flame over the cords. They glowed incandescently, but when he ceased blowing flame, the glow faded, leaving the red strings intact. His heart sank, but Cherith, who'd dried her tears to watch, gasped, clutching Mak's fingers.

"Mak! I think I have the answer!" Her eyes brimmed with excitement. "Remember how we vanquished the Nageen!"

DeMaksim stared at her. "You pushed water, I spat fire and they ..." A grin split his face. "Together! Our powers combined and we overcame her together. Of course!"

"Ready?" Cherith grinned up at him. "Now!" Cherith flicked her fingers, creating and throwing magical water while DeMaksim breathed fire at it. A sizzling blue-green wave of icy arctic foam hit the Nageen's rubbery mating strings – turning them crystalline and solid.

Dario gaped.

Becks whooped. "You've turned it to ice!"

"Yes!" DeMaksim crowed. "And ice breaks." He urged Cherith closer to the metal cooking pot and smashed their iced wrists against its lip. Shattering, the ice fell away and the strings were gone as if they'd never been, leaving them unrestrained individuals once more.

"We're free!" Cherith squealed. She flung herself at Mak, grabbing him around the neck with both hands. Mak firmed his arms around her waist and danced them in a circle before stopping to take her in a sweeping kiss. Only easing back when they needed to breathe, DeMaksim became aware of the grinning crowd. Family members and other Fae, including Queen Maerovana, had gathered, drawn by the excitement.

"Congratulations!" The queen smiled.

As the congratulations died down, the queen pulled them aside. "It was serendipitous the Nageen caught you with her mating strings, despite the problems it caused."

"Yes," DeMaksim said, smiling down at his mate. "Although, I still don't understand how her spell lasted so strongly after her death."

"Ah," the queen nodded sagely. "I think I do. It's because they're imbued with a small part of her life essence just before they're cast; only the Nageen can recall her essence, but having died, she couldn't, leaving the life essence to continue carrying out its programme, to the best of its minimal ability. The entrapment of two people was an added complication it was incapable of dealing with."

"Oh!" Cherith shuddered. "Kind of sad in a way, like she was haunting us."

DeMaksim snorted. "A mindless parasite can't become a ghost, All Hallows' Eve or not."

Cherith shrugged. "No matter now. She and her influence are gone, something we achieved as a team."

"You did." The Queen smiled. "You excel together – true mates, I believe?"

"Yes!" They laughed because they'd spoken in unison.

"Excellent." Queen Maerovana nodded. "I recognise and accept your true mating – we'll have a ball in the not-too-distant future so that you can dance the Rhynfallia and seal the deal." She cleared her throat. "Meanwhile, I've decided you two are the perfect replacement for that traitorous fool, Eskavon. I can't waste any time sorting this out, so I hereby pronounce you River Queen Cherith and Dracon River King DeMaksim – joint rulers of the Mirkdowd River and all tributaries from this moment forth." She raised both hands, placing one on Cherith's chest and one on Mak's chest. From that link, power snapped into place, arcing through them and bowing their bodies. It shot from their pores and out in a growing radius to arc over the suffering Water Fae and rain down upon them in a shower of sparks which were thirstily absorbed into their skins. The change was immediate; Fae-folk crying out in joy, hands on their chests, rejoicing over their restored links to the river and their new rulers.

Cherith focused on DeMaksim, her expression creased with worry. "Mak! You're no longer heir of the Papillion duchy – are you okay with that?"

Framing Cherith's face in his, DeMaksim smiled at his gorgeous mate. "It'll take some getting used to, but the position will just have to move on to one of my siblings." He caressed her cheeks. "I love you, Cherith. You're the person I never knew I needed until I found you in the river and I'll spend the rest of our lives proving it, wherever we are. You complete me."

"Oh, Mak." Cherith nuzzled into the hand cupping her cheek. "I love you, too. To think you, my Seelie Spy, turned out to be my true mate. How many times we've cursed the Nageen and yet, the queen is right: if it wasn't for her tying us together, we might never have guessed the truth."

DeMaksim laughed. "Somehow we would've, darling, I'm sure of it." He kissed her briefly. "But I can honestly say, I'll be happy to never see a Nageen again for as long as I live."

Cherith's aqua eyes sparkled at him. "I'll dance to that."

And they did.

The End.

~ THE END ~

Thank you for reading Cherith and DeMaksim's story. I hope you enjoyed it. If you'd like to find out what happens next, then I recommend Lyssica and Emryn's story!

Find it here:
Blizzards and Beginnings

ACKNOWLEDGMENTS

This story is loosely based on traditional fairy tales. There are no mistakes, only design changes and my imagination.

I would like to thank:

- Everyone who encouraged me to write this story.
- My fellow Anthology authors: Leisl, Marnie and Samantha
- All my readers
- My daughter Samantha for her constant love and assistance
- My puppy-dog Lexie for her continual devotion and her desire to sit in my lap, even when I'm typing
- My kettle for providing numerous cups of tea
- My chocolate stash for its persistent nagging

IF YOU LOVED THIS ONE...

Please leave a review!

Reviews really help authors; it directs our books into the right kind of hands, which in turn allows me to keep writing more books for you to enjoy.

So, if you had a blast reading this story, I'd be ever so grateful if you left a review wherever you can.

Thank you!
♥

ALSO BY HELLUCY HOWE

What would you do if winter grew teeth and claws?

Lady Lyssica Aphiski, unexpected heir to the Duke of Papillion, is driven to prove to her father she is capable of fulfilling her role – even if it means juggling her estate duties with her secret and sacred responsibility as Handmaiden to the Unseelie Goddess, Ostara. Everything is going swimmingly until the first snow of winter arrives weeks ahead of schedule. If that wasn't enough, the participants for the Tri-moon training program arrive, bringing with them a scourge from Lyssica's past.

When Lord Emryn Phengaris agreed to represent his Changeling Clan in the Tri-moon program, he had no idea he'd end up as personal bodyguard to the gorgeous Lady Lyssica Aphiski. To make matters worse, his animal side insists she's their mate, which is impossible because, despite his fascination with her steel spine and shimmering smile, she's not changeling.

Then a Tri-moon apprentice is murdered by an ancient evil determined to bring about eternal winter. Only one thing stands in his way – the magic Lyssica has kept secret since childhood. With her world thrown into chaos and danger at every turn, Emryn proves the anchor Lyssica never knew she needed. Together, they must find the strength to vanquish not only the demons threatening the Queendom, but the ones inside their hearts.

Read on for a sneak preview of Chapter One!

CHAPTER ONE

LYSSICA

*F*ace pressed to the window, Lady Lyssica Aphiski stared at the soft falling snow, a moue of dismay twisting her mouth. Each new flake drifted on the wind's sigh, before inexorably dropping to freshen the ground's rapidly whitening carpet.

Winter's first snow? Already?

The frosty evidence was undeniable, even though leaves remained on most trees, and Juberd, the first moon of winter, was yet two weeks away.

"Goddess blast it." Lyssica pressed frustrated fingers to the glass – the tips forming claws – as if she could grab fistfuls of the wet stuff and somehow dispose of it. The early seasonal change would play havoc with the Duchy's horticultural plans; she'd have to adapt her timelines, bring some tasks forward and postpone others. Biting her bottom lip, she fought to swallow annoyance at firm evidence of the Cailleach's impatience to launch her season. But would she want to maintain the balance and leave early at winter's end? Lyssica huffed a laugh. Winter's Queen had never been known for half measures, but perhaps she'd entered into an agreement with Modron, the Autumn Goddess.

Swinging back to her mirror, Lyssica thrust more jewelled pins into her chignon. It was as well the Tri-moon apprentices were arriving today, because, if snow continued, travel would become difficult. Speaking of – she needed to hurry, or the apprentices would arrive at the front door before she did, and wouldn't Papan be thrilled about that?

The chignon's upsweep captured her wild mass of ebony hair, although the swathe of emerald above her left temple and swirl of lavender near her right ear were still prominent. If she turned her head, she'd see cobalt streaks which—

The antique Godfather clock in the downstairs antechamber gonged, the reverberations clanging through her revery. *Shite, Lyssica, get a move on!* Snatching up her makeup kit, she flicked it open and grabbed an applicator.

"Tig, could you please bring my mulberry cling-boots from the dressing room?" The words had barely left her lips when Antigony Lyonetti appeared in the mirror's background; her hair slightly dishevelled, but mouth curved with satisfaction, she brandished said footwear, trophy style.

"One step ahead of you, Lady Lyss."

"Excellent." Lyssica swept blush powder across her cheeks, pausing to contemplate the effect. Nodded. The peach was the perfect colour for her. Using a fingertip, she framed her aquamarine eyes with kohl and the lids with glimmering deep purple before wiping her fingers clean with a soft cloth. Smoothing her fitted violet silken shell, she assessed her outfit; the golden accents on the tunic-length garment went a long way to elevate the outfit from stark simplicity. Just below her hips, the tailored violet and gold trousers flowed down her legs to bell slightly around the lower leg and cuff at the ankle. "What do you think, Tig? I'm trying to look like a professional without losing femininity." She twisted this way and that.

"Everyone will fall at your feet, Lady Lyss." Antigony nodded as she proffered the shin-high boots. "And these will be the perfect finishing touch. Your Papan can't fail to be impressed."

Lyssica grimaced. "Let's hope you're right."

Rattling noises had Antigony hurrying to the window. "Carriages coming up the driveway Lady Lyss!"

"Goddess blast it!" Lyssica slid one foot into a boot, tabbing the side clasp shut as she hobbled for the stairway.

"Your cloak, milady!" Antigony chased after her, the indigo-coloured velvet garment held wide. Glancing back, Lyssica was startled by the cloak's resemblance to a storm sweeping in, then the soft folds enveloped her and the gold fastener clicked into place at her throat.

"Thanks, Tig." She reeled down the tower staircase, the cloak billowing. At the bottom, Lyssica clutched the railing with one hand, lifted her stocking clad foot, positioned her boot, fumbled with the buckle and – hissed as it slipped from her grasp.

"Hell's horns!" Closing her eyes, she mentally counted out her frustration ... *One duskit, two bunnies, three squizzles and – everything's fine, so slow the hell down.* Opening her eyes, she discovered Entanglit, the Papillion Estate's major-domo, proffering her errant boot.

A smile stretched her lips. "Thank you, Entanglit." She wobbled to a nearby chair, sat, thrust her foot inside and tabbed it closed. Regaining her feet, she hastened out through the foyer to the wide, wisteria-entwined verandah.

Maman's face lit up. "There you are, Lyssica sweetie. You're looking lovely."

Papan, the almighty Duke Yanvian Aphiski, flicked her a stern glance. "Beginning to think you wouldn't make it. The carriages are close."

Lyssica clenched her teeth. Convincing him to accept her as heir, a position left empty by her brother, DeMaksim, departing on Joint Queendom business, was something she'd had to fight for – and continued to – on a daily basis. Drumming her fingers on the porch railing, she refused to dignify Papan's barb with an answer, but memories flooded in.

Papan's refusal to include a nineteen-year-old Lyssica in the estate management lessons alongside DeMaksim. "You are a Fae-female and a lady. The position is above your ability."

"But I want to learn, Papan."

"You misunderstand me, Lyssica. Young ladies don't have the capability or intelligence. Stay within your limits and enjoy yourself."

The words had stung like darts; sharp stabs flaying her skin, allowing the polluted slime of hurt and anger to seep out. Reacting to the poison, she'd taken his advice and gone on a pleasure-seeking spree. Flirting with anything male, drinking to excess and partying her days away – boring but harmless, until she'd fallen victim to a predator.

She sighed, hating the idea of reliving those memories; afterwards, the only thing to save her from her self-loathing and heartache was her sworn oath to the Goddess Ostara. Completing the promised daily ritual became the light of her life, keeping her afloat in a quagmire of toxic ooze where her companions turned out to be users and abusers and her father thought her nothing but a pretty frippery.

It wasn't really his fault, she knew. The Seelie Fae had been a patriarchal society for thousands of years despite being ruled by a Queen. Stupid really. The Unseelie Fae weren't so ridiculously hidebound. Secretly, Lyssica had always admired their attitude. If you possessed the power or the skill, the Unseelie didn't care if you were female, male, or of some alternate persuasion. If you could do the job, it was win-win and you were in.

But things had recently begun to change and the uniting of the Queendoms under singular joint rule was a sign of new times ahead.

She hoped.

Despite the fact that Seelie and Unseelie were now supposed to be one, the changes went against the traditions of several hundred years and there were those who struggled with the new status quo; and some who openly rebelled.

"This first Tri-moon program is very important." Duke

Yanvian's voice brought her back to the moment at hand. Lyssica listened. Kind of. She'd heard it all before. A nearby grime-rose bush was much more interesting. Were the leaves bruised?

He waved a hand. "The level of success we attain will set the tone for the programs of future years."

Well accustomed to her father's love of rambling lectures, Lyssica reached to cup a leaf in her hand and was startled into dropping it when electricity zapped her palm. Mouth agape, she stared at the faint leafy imprint singed into her soft skin, then blew on her hand and shook it briskly.

Papan nodded, rocking back on his heels, as usual, completely oblivious to the fact she wasn't fully listening. "So everything we say and do must be carefully thought out in advance."

She peered at the plant – was there a blue glow overshadowing it? Instinctively, she began humming; leaning over the railing as she sang faintly, aiming her goddess power at the roots of the grime-rose bush. It sizzled, so she crooned a few more words of healing and encouragement.

Papan twisted, hands snapping to hips. "Lyssica! Are you even listening?"

The trembling bush sagged, before her quiet words imbued strength and life back into it. Then it brightened. She turned her head, regarded him coolly. "Absolutely Papan. As always you make perfect sense."

A few feet away, Maman chuckled. "You're always humming and singing. I never quite hear what you're singing about, but the plants seem to love your voice. It's no wonder our Papillion Duchy gardens are admired and envied by visitors."

Lyssica stiffened, flicked her mother an innocent glance. Did Maman suspect something? She dug her nails into her palms. That wouldn't do. "Oh? You think they hear and respond, Maman?" She laughed. "It's not very likely, but wouldn't it be fantastic? I'd adore being able to help them like that." She did adore it. "But really, it's just our marvellous gardening staff and my fancies. When I tell the plants how beautiful they are, surely they understand?"

She didn't admit how much of the gardens' beauty actually was due to her nurturing. Couldn't admit it even if she wanted to; Ostara had enspelled Lyssica's silence for her own protection.

But Lyssica found there were folk who wanted a reason for everything. *'You must have a green thumb!'* Was a comment she'd heard several times, when her thumb had nothing to do with it – the wonderful results were a direct response to the use of her goddess-given power. Her *Unseelie* goddess-given power. In a territory where the worshipped spring deity had always been the Seelie Goddess, Olwen, Lyssica was a handmaiden of Ostara.

Her father's hand clasping her arm jolted her into the moment. "Stop that infernal singing and look sharp; we've a reputation to uphold, Lyssica."

She wrenched her arm free and, holding her father's gaze, pointed. "Those plants aren't thriving in this early cold snap. Last night's snowfall was untimely, and unnatural."

Duke Yanvian beetled his brows. "Maybe Modron, the Autumn Goddess, wanted to leave early, she is female after all. The phrase 'changeable as the weather' is often used to describe the unsettled minds of females; neither easily explained. Early winters are never a good thing for crops and everyone will be in the same predicament. We can't be held accountable for the weather, Lyssica. We'll do the best we can."

Lyssica clasped her fingers together tightly. "Heavy snow three weeks early has nothing to do with the workings of female minds. With what promises to be a harsh winter looming, forage in the forest will diminish quickly and survival for any living being will become difficult."

"Oh, don't worry." Duke Yanvian waved a hand as the first carriage floated to a stop at the base of the colonnaded portico, popped out supporting legs, and settled. The second conveyance drifted to a stop and planted itself close behind. "We'll feed any deer seeking shelter on the estate, as we've always done."

Lyssica bit her lip; she worried for more than the deer, but their argument must wait. Below them, carriage doors opened, their inbuilt steps automatically descending. Shivering, she clutched at the edges of her velvet cloak; her dracon genetics responded to her unconscious prompt and upped her internal furnace until the cold vanished from her system. Smoothing her hands down her tunic, she drew a deep breath. Winter wasn't going to leave and neither were the new arrivals.

The candidates were engaging in the programme of reciprocal sponsorships discussed and approved at the last United Queendom's Summer Council. Selected single adult children of participating families were to spend the three moons of winter as apprentices at other properties. Some larger estates had accepted several apprentices and agreed to send more than one of their offspring elsewhere. It was embraced as a way to extend skills, promote cooperation, encourage friendships and see if any parties located suitable mates or consorts. Lyssica grimaced; a training program yes, but also a marriage market. Now, five Fae-males and one Fae-female stood on the lower steps.

Duchesse Azura entwined her gloved hands. "I hope our girls have arrived at their destinations safely."

Her consort flashed her a smile. "I'm certain they have. You needn't worry so, my dear." His smile faded. "It's a pity Trey refused. I think it would've benefitted him."

The Duchesse tilted her hand, palm upward. "You know he can't process things on short notice. At least he agreed to join next year's program."

Duke Yanvian nodded. "Better than absolute repudiation, which we all know he's capable of."

Their Tri-moon guests climbed the steps, their features becoming easier to pick out. Staring in consternation, Lyssica tuned her parents out. *Is that...? No, surely not.* But it was. In the advancing group were two faces she'd wished never to see again. Lord Perris Momphiday and Lord Venaday Tortrician. The first regarded her with a sly smile and one elevated eyebrow, the second rubbed his hands while grinning hugely.

Shite, bugger, and hell's horns! *I'm going to be sick.* No, no, she wouldn't. She couldn't. Swallowing harshly, she tried to rope in her errant emotions and thoughts. *Should have paid more attention when Papan showed me the lists! At least I'd have been more prepared. Maybe.* She dug fingernails into palms. *Don't look at him.* She turned her attention to the other four Fae-folk. She didn't recognise any of them; their wings were either tightly furled against the snow or tucked under cloaks so she there were no wing markings to help her.

Duke Yanvian spread his hands. "Welcome all!"

Duchesse Azura smiled widely. "You must be chilled. Let's retire to the salon for refreshments. The house is infinitely warmer."

Lyssica forced a smile. "So pleased." *Not.* At least, not to see— She shook her head internally. "Don't worry about your luggage, it will be taken to your rooms."

Cutting ruthlessly across the path of his companions to halt in front of her, Lord Venaday swept Lyssica a bow. "Lady Lyssica! Such a thrill to be in your delightful company again. Perhaps we can play cards as we used to? You remember the 'Swig or Strip' parties, don't you?"

"Oh! I can't say I do." *More than I'd like to.* "Are you sure I was involved? We were all very young back then and these days my time is filled with important tasks." Lyssica forced a smile. "As I'm certain your life is, Lord Venaday. I hope we have all changed and matured."

"Not too much change, I hope," he said, waggling his brows at her before moving to follow her mother.

Left by herself, Lyssica wasn't certain whether to laugh hysterically, hiss with anger, or cry in despair. Of course, she couldn't do any of those until she was safely back in her room and away from — She shuddered then pinched the bridge of her nose. How was she going to go in there and pretend like everything was normal?

Goddess help me, please. A zing shot through her body, electrifying every hair; she was left with the uneasy feeling that her words had been answered.

But what was her answer?

～

Want to find out what happens next?
Grab your copy here:
Blizzards and Beginnings
(Currently only available as part of the anthology *A Perfectly Paranormal Easter*)

OTHER TALES BY HELLUCY HOWE

~

The Fae Courts

A sweeping fantasy romance series filled with fae, gods, magic… and plenty of adventure!

A Perfectly Paranormal Anthologies

A collection of paranormal romance anthologies in conjunction with several other wonderful authors.

~

To find out more about any of these, visit my website:

www.hellucywrites.com

PART OF THE TRIBE

I love to hear from, and keep in touch with, fellow book worms! If you'd like to spend a little more time together, you can find me in the following places:

FACEBOOK

- A Perfectly Paranormal Anthologies Reader Group - Perfectly Paranormal Paramours

Or send me an email at - hellucywrites@gmail.com - I love hearing from readers and authors alike!

ABOUT THE AUTHOR

Meet Hellucy Howe, a Book Dragon who teethed on romantic fairy tales and went on to voraciously devour anything paranormal. Writing was also second nature but became something to do in secret when the stories of her young child mind were ridiculed. Homes were populated with books and hidden caches of story notebooks inspired by a fertile brain and a massive creative streak.

She became a Professional Reader and a Closet Scribbler, convinced no one would want to look at the mad ramblings of someone who hates getting dirt under her fingernails and knows ironing was invented as a torture method.

Nowadays, Helen loves inventing paranormal and fantasy romance from the comfort of her cosy study with a hot cup of tea beside her laptop and her little spaniel, Lexie, snoring at her feet. With her anthology contribution of 'Filigree and Fate', Helen has been dragged kicking and screaming from her closet, into the deer-in-headlights world of being a Real Author.

www.ingramcontent.com/pod-product-compliance
Lightning Source LLC
Chambersburg PA
CBHW030637120726
47904CB00006B/2191